CHASING SECRETS

ALSO BY GENNIFER CHOLDENKO

Al Capone Does My Shirts

Al Capone Does My Homework

Al Capone Shines My Shoes

No Passengers Beyond This Point

If a Tree Falls at Lunch Period

Notes from a Liar and Her Dog

CHASING SECRETS

GENNIFER CHOLDENKO

WENDY
LAMB
BOOKS

 Published in the United States by Wendy Lamb Books, an imprint of Random House Children's Books, a division of Random House LLC, a Penguin Random House Company, New York.

Wendy Lamb Books and the colophon are trademarks of Random House LLC.

Visit us on the Web! randomhousekids.com

Educators and librarians, for a variety of teaching tools, visit us at RHTeachersLibrarians.com

Library of Congress Cataloging-in-Publication Data
Choldenko, Gennifer, author.
Chasing secrets / Gennifer Choldenko. — First edition.
pages cm
Summary: Thirteen-year-old Lizzie and her secret friend Noah, who is hiding in her house, plan to rescue Noah's father from the quarantined Chinatown, and save everyone they love from contracting the plague that is spreading in 1900 San Francisco.
ISBN 978-0-385-74253-5 (trade) — ISBN 978-0-375-99063-2 (lib. bdg.) — ISBN 978-0-385-74254-2 (pbk.) — ISBN 978-0-307-97577-5 (ebook)
1. Plague—Juvenile fiction. 2. Friendship—Juvenile fiction. 3. Fathers and daughters—Juvenile fiction. 4. Quarantine—Juvenile fiction. 5. Chinese—Juvenile fiction. 6. San Francisco (Calif.)—Juvenile fiction. [1. Plague—Fiction. 2. Friendship—Fiction. 3. Quarantine—Fiction. 4. Chinese Americans—Fiction. 5. San Francisco (Calif.)—History—20th century—Fiction.] I. Title.
PZ7.C446265Ch 2015
[Fic]—dc23
2014040329

The text of this book is set in 13-point Adobe Garamond Pro.
Jacket design by Kate Gartner
Interior design by Stephanie Moss

Printed in the United States of America
10 9 8 7 6 5 4 3 2 1
First Edition

To Kai—who knew it would
be so fun to have a daughter?

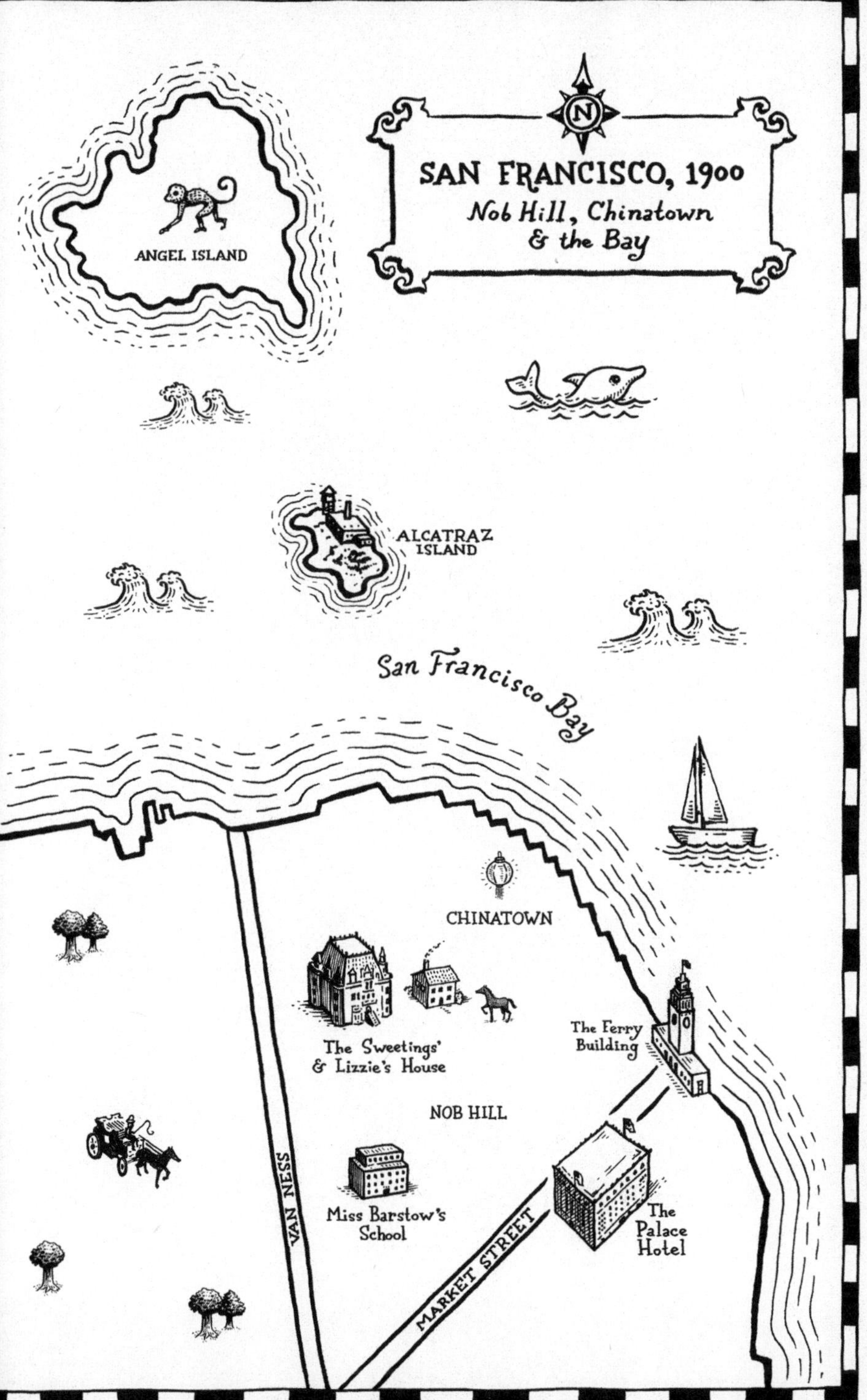
SAN FRANCISCO, 1900
Nob Hill, Chinatown
& the Bay
N
ANGEL ISLAND
ALCATRAZ
ISLAND
San Francisco Bay
CHINATOWN
The Sweetings'
& Lizzie's House
The Ferry
Building
NOB HILL
Miss Barstow's
School
VAN NESS
MARKET STREET
The
Palace
Hotel

SAN FRANCISCO, JANUARY 1, 1900

In the Palace Hotel, electric lights blaze as ladies in shimmering gowns and gentlemen in black waistcoats waltz in a ballroom gilded with gold. On the cobblestones of Market Street, revelers jangle cowbells to ring in the new century for the city, the Pearl of the Pacific.

In the bay, a steamer from Honolulu is fumigated, scrubbed, and smoked—from the silk-seated parlors to the stinking steerage—and given entry to the port of San Francisco.

At the dock, thick with the smell of fish, rats slip off the ship. They scurry onto the wharf and climb the sewers to Chinatown.

One.

Two.

Three.

Four.

PART ONE

The Cook, the Maid, Our Horse, and Papa

I find a spot on the bench in front of the line of carriages, buggies, and one stalled motorcar facing the wrong direction, trying my best to ignore the other girls' whispered plans as they climb into each other's buggies after school. They're going to wear split skirts and bicycle in Golden Gate Park, or carry parasols and wear hats and gloves to shop at the Emporium, or go to each other's houses to try on new cotillion dresses. I crack open my book as more girls sweep by. A book is a friend you take with you wherever you go.

Gemma leans on her crutches next to the bench, resting her black-stockinged toe on the ground. Her sprained ankle is bandaged in a crisscross pattern—very different from the way my father does it. Gemma has blue eyes, reddish-blond hair, and full cheeks that always look feverish. "What are you reading about?"

"Mucus," I tell her. "Did you know your nose produces a flask full of mucus every day?"

Gemma makes a face. "A flask full . . . Don't tell me you drink it?"

"Actually, I do. Everyone does." I know I shouldn't say things like this. Aunt Hortense says I try hard to be peculiar. But she's wrong; I come by it quite naturally.

"Did Spencer ask you yet?" Hattie with the pouty lips calls to Gemma.

Gemma turns to answer. I don't hear what she says. It isn't intended for me. Nothing they say ever is.

It's been a long time since I've had a friend my age. I should be used to it by now. I was eleven when Aunt Hortense insisted I enroll in Miss Barstow's School for Young Women, where every girl learns the virtues of patience, the proper use of calling cards, and how to marry a man of stature, which means he has money. Last year, Clara, my friend from church, moved away, and my big brother, Billy, turned mean and stopped letting me tag along with him.

Now I'm thirteen, and my friends are the cook, the maid, our horse, and my father. Luckily, tomorrow I get to go on calls with Papa, so I won't have to face Miss Barstow's for three whole days. I've been assisting my father for only a few months, but I've taken to it like butter to biscuits.

What Papa does is a lot more interesting than what we learn in school. There's no science at Miss Barstow's. No math after third grade. We take subjects deemed necessary for cultured young women destined to run a household of servants—French, elocution, dancing, music, geography, etiquette, and entertaining.

I like geography the best, then French and elocution. Etiquette and entertaining put me to sleep, and dancing is pure agony.

When I look up again, Jing is here in our black buggy with our filly, Juliet, who's snorting and prancing like she hasn't been out in a while.

Jing waggles his eyebrows at me, and I climb up beside him.

He flaps the reins, and Juliet trots forward into the street. Bits of foam fly where the lines rub against her shiny brown neck.

Jing doesn't have a long braid or wear baggy pants and white socks the way most Chinamen do. He dresses like my father and speaks formally, never in pidgin English. We say he's our cook, but he also takes care of our garden, our two horses, our nine chickens, and our cat, Orange Tom. But not the parrot, Mr. P. Our maid, Maggy Doyle, looks after Mr. P. Maggy does the work of three maids, but she has peculiar ways. "Addled," Billy calls her.

We take the route by the sign that says PAINLESS PIANO-PLAYING DENTIST. Painless, my foot. Papa says he plays the piano so no one can hear his patients scream.

Jing smiles slyly. "See anything in my ear?"

I lean in. "No."

He turns his head. "How about the other one?"

I peer in that ear. "Nope."

"Ahhh . . . what's this?" He pretends to pull a tiny frog out of his right ear and hands it to me.

I grin at him, inspecting the live frog in my hand. It's bright green with a black mask.

Jing always has something for me. A smooth black stone, a white feather or cookies baked in the shape of my initials. I keep his gifts on my windowsill, except for the ones I eat.

He asks me how Miss Barstow's was today, and I try to think of a story that will make him laugh.

"Miss Barstow bought a new dunce cap. She tried it on to demonstrate what will happen if you flunk your French vocabulary test, but her hairpin got caught and she couldn't get it off. Miss Annabelle had to help her."

"Stuck dumb," Jing says.

"Dumbstuck," I say, and laugh. "It serves her right. I hate that thing. Not that I've ever had to wear it, but still."

We pass a workhorse pulling a big dray. On the corner, white-ribboned temperance ladies pass out flyers, and newsboys hawk papers.

"Orange Tom has disappeared again. I have a hunch he has a lady friend," Jing says.

The frog hops in my lap. I cup my hand over him to prevent escape. "I hope his lady friend likes rats."

Orange Tom loves to hunt, but he kills more than he can eat. He's fond of leaving dead rodents in Aunt Hortense's fountain, in the backseat of Uncle Karl's brand-new automachine, on our front step, and on top of Papa's medical journals.

The farther we get from Miss Barstow's, the more my mood improves. I settle back and enjoy the short ride up the hill to home.

Aunt Hortense and Uncle Karl's house on Nob Hill is enormous—five times the size of ours—and built to look like a palace in Paris. Crystal chandeliers, paintings of angels, marble busts of famous old men, gold candelabras held up by gold cupids with gold twigs in their gold hands. Every night it's lit with all electric light.

Aunt Hortense and Uncle Karl own our house, which is tiny compared to theirs but plenty large enough for Papa, Billy, and me. Aunt Hortense married sugar money. Her sister, Lucy, my mother, married a doctor who will care for patients whether they can pay or not.

My mother died five years ago. It started with a stomachache; Papa thought she had parasites, but it was cancer. No cure for that. Maybe I will discover one.

When my father is away on calls, Aunt Hortense steps in to oversee Maggy, Jing, Billy, and me. I've tried to convince Papa that now that Billy is sixteen, he should be in charge. Billy is bad-tempered, but I still prefer him to Aunt Hortense. I haven't been able to persuade Papa yet.

Aunt Hortense never lets up—I'm not to come or go without her permission. I guess it's because she can't have children of her own that she thinks she owns us.

I watch her walk down the steps from her house, wearing a yellow dress that sounds like a bristle brush when she walks. She has on white lace-up boots and carries a pearl-handled parasol. Most of her clothes come from Paris. A few weeks a year, French dresses are brought to the Fairmont Hotel for ladies to purchase.

Jing reins in Juliet so I can climb out. I like it better when I get to help unharness her, but I can't do that with Aunt Hortense standing here.

I still have the frog in my hand, and contemplate handing it to her. How she'd jump! Aunt Hortense is terrified of amphibians and reptiles. She's allergic to cats and doesn't like dogs.

She peers at me. "Oh, for goodness' sake, Elizabeth. What did you do to your hair?"

"Trimmed it, ma'am."

"With a meat cleaver? They have better hairstyles at the almshouse."

"Really? Well, I'll sign myself up," I say under my breath.

"I heard that," Aunt Hortense snaps. "Don't you know what a privilege it is to go to Miss Barstow's? What did *she* say about your hair?"

"That I ought to keep it pinned up."

My father comes out the kitchen door with his brown medical bag in his right hand and his black bag in his left. Papa is tall, like me, with hair the color of piecrust, and brown eyes like mine.

"Hurry and change, Lizzie. I just got word Mrs. Jessen is having her baby," Papa says.

Aunt Hortense frowns. "Must you take her with you, Jules? It was bad enough when you took William."

"She likes going."

"Where do the Jessens live?" Aunt Hortense asks.

"Larkspur."

"Larkspur? She'll miss school tomorrow."

"She'll make up what she missed, won't you, Lizzie?" Papa asks.

"Yes, sir." I lean down to hide my smile, release the frog, and then run up the path to our house.

Aunt Hortense shakes her head at Papa. "Even so, Jules . . ."

"It's okay, Aunt Hortense. Childbirth is not contagious," I call back.

"I'm just trying to keep you safe, Elizabeth. Don't you know that?"

The Doctor's Daughter

Jing drives us to the ferry. In the sky, plumes of yellow smoke shoot up from Chinatown. The air is yellow and smells of rotten eggs and burning trash. I'm glad we aren't going that way.

We've just pulled up to the dock when I spot Billy. Billy looks like Mama in Papa's extra large size. He has her dark hair, and eyes so blue, they're almost violet. He doesn't have huge feet the way I do, but he has big hands—each the size of a loaf of bread. Aunt Hortense has to send to New York to get gloves that fit. Apparently New York is full of people with big hands.

Billy has his jacket off and his shirtsleeves rolled up. He's headed toward a crowd of young men watching a street fight. I raise my arm to wave, then yank it back. Our father won't be happy Billy is down here. If I say hello, Billy will accuse me of telling Papa on him.

I watch Papa out of the corner of my eye; he hasn't spotted Billy. But the way Jing's eyebrows move, I'm pretty sure *he* has.

After the ferry ride across the choppy green water, Papa and I rent a horse and buggy from the livery. Just as we climb up, the rain begins to come down. By the time we dig our slickers out, we're soaked. The wind howls; water and mud splash up from the road. Steam rises from the warm horses. Even with a hat on, my hair is dripping wet by the time we tie the horse outside the Jessens' little house and tramp inside.

Luckily, Papa knows Mrs. Jessen. Some ladies would rather die than have a strange doctor examine them.

In the small cabin, Mrs. Jessen's five-year-old daughter, Caroline, stands holding her swollen misshapen arm. Her mother is screaming like her hair is caught in the hooves of a galloping horse.

Papa has an established order of who to help first—triage, he calls it. Children, then women, then old men, then young men. But who comes first in this case? The baby inside Mrs. Jessen, or Caroline? There are no grandmothers hovering, no hired men in the yard, no neighbors offering a helping hand. Nobody but Caroline Jessen, her mother, my father, and me.

Papa carefully inspects Caroline's arm. "It's a fracture. How'd you hurt it, little one?"

"Fell," Caroline whispers.

"My daughter, Lizzie, will take good care of you," he tells her gently, then turns his attention to Mrs. Jessen as he talks me through setting Caroline's arm.

"Get some chloroform and the gauze mask. Come show me when you have it," he calls.

This is more than he's asked of me before. Did he forget I'm only thirteen?

"Move, Lizzie!" he shouts.

Mrs. Jessen's screams are gaining on us like the whistle of an oncoming train.

Papa has two doctor bags: the black satchel full of medicine, the brown one packed with instruments wrapped in soft cloth. The chloroform is in the black one, along with mustard poultices, camphor, ammonia, liniment, and rubbing alcohol. I dig through the brown bag, looking for the gauze mask under the bandages—old sheets cut and rolled by Jing.

When I don't find the mask, I plow through again, making a mess of things. Papa isn't going to like this. But then I feel the cool smooth edge of metal . . . the mask.

Papa sees I have it. "Is there a piece of wood around? Three inches by seven?"

"Seven inches. Do we have a ruler?" I ask.

"Just guess. You'll use it as a brace." His voice is calm and encouraging, but I know he won't be happy if I make a mistake.

I head outside. The rain has let up. It's misting now, the water hanging in the air. My boots stick in the mud, making a sucking sound as I pull them out.

I run to the boathouse and then cut around the back. The boat's paddles are on one side, firmly attached to the boat hut. They're too large. Besides, I can't get them off.

The terror in Caroline's eyes makes my mind spin like a bicycle wheel with no chain attached.

In the reeds stands an egret, slender and elegant. I watch it and try to calm myself. Where am I going to find something to use as a brace?

No trees; it's all marsh here. Monterey pines grow in the back, behind the house, but they are full of gnarly branches. We need something flat.

The egret lifts its pterodactyl wings and takes off, its thin legs dangling behind. And there—just beyond the bird—I see a broken oar in the reeds. I trudge through the muck, tug the paddle pieces from the mud. There is one about the right size! I wash it in the bay, the water sloping into my boots. Then I run up to the house to boil water. Papa makes me boil everything.

On the porch, I notice a spittoon, along with small cages of animals. Mice, squirrels, a raccoon.

In the back room, Papa has clean sheets and towels around Mrs. Jessen. He's talking to her in that comforting way he has.

Caroline is huddled in the corner of the front room, her brown hair matted with snarls and snot, her eyes wide. A pulse beats in her small forehead. My father says a patient must have faith in you. But how do you earn trust? If Caroline is anything like the girls at school, I'm in big trouble.

"You're going to be fine," I say.

"Get away," she spits.

Papa has his hands full with Mrs. Jessen. If Caroline runs from me, there's no way I can get the metal form with the gauze mask over her nose so that I can pour the chloroform one drop at a time. Papa instructed me precisely how to use it—chloroform can be deadly.

I move closer. Her arm hangs like a Z. How can an arm look like that?

"You ain't a doctor." Her whole body caves around her arm, protecting it from me.

"I can do this. I've done it before," I lie.

"Leave me alone. My father's a policeman," Caroline kicks out at me, her foot catching air.

"Calm her down," Papa calls from the back room. "Then give her the chloroform, *carefully*!"

Caroline cowers behind an old loom. "Stay away."

My eyes search the house for clues about her. Then I remember the animals on the porch. "What is your raccoon's name?"

She won't answer.

"Is your papa a policeman in Larkspur?" I ask.

"San Francisco." I can barely hear her over her mother's moans. Tears flood Caroline's eyes.

Then I understand. Caroline is more afraid for her mother than she is for herself. I know how that feels. For a split second I feel a sting, because Caroline's mother is here with her and mine is dead. Then I whisper, "He won't hurt her."

Caroline quivers. "He's hurtin' her now!"

"She's having a baby. It hurts a lot. But he'll help her. He knows how." I work at making my voice comforting.

The tears spill down Caroline's cheeks, making pink lines in her dirty face. "No," she hiccups, her shoulders convulsing, but her eyes are watching me.

"Yes," I say. "It's always this way. It's painful when the baby comes." I try to sound calm. I've never attended a childbirth before, but I know this much.

Caroline eyes me. "God's doing this to her?"

"No. God's taking care of her. Some things in life just hurt. But your mama's in good hands now."

I sense her agreeing with me more than I see it.

"My papa is a good doctor. He'll bring her through this."

Her eyes absorb this.

"He will. He's delivered hundreds of babies. He knows what he's doing," I say as I pray for a normal birth.

She nods. The hand of her good arm creeps forward, finger by finger to touch me.

I take the last step to her, wiping the hair gently from her face.

So Many Dead Rats

We're up half the night, pulling a small person out of Mrs. Jessen, which is like getting a boulder out of a pickle jar. Impossible . . . but somehow it happens.

After my father finishes cleaning the afterbirth, the creature looks more like a baby and less like a gnome. Papa says they don't cry much the first day, but this baby's cries pierce holes in my eardrums. My father isn't right about everything.

Mr. Jessen is home now, out back chopping wood in the morning light. Mrs. Jessen and the new baby, Thomas, are sound asleep. I was asleep, too, curled up in a chair, when Papa woke me. "We have to get going, or we'll owe another day's charge for the buggy."

Mr. Jessen is a big man with a hearty handshake. "Much

obliged, Lizzie," he tells me when he comes through the door, bringing in the smell of chopped wood.

"Looks like you got yourself some help there," Papa says, and nods toward the back bedroom.

Mr. Jessen grins. "Gonna be a while before I can get much work out of him."

"True enough, but he's got a fine set of lungs. I can vouch for that."

"That he does. Thanks, Jules. I know it's a slog for you to come all the way out here. But given what's been going on in the city, the farther away the better."

"Something I should know about?"

"Restaurant down on Sutter stinks to high heaven. Got incense burning to mask the smell. Finally opened up the wall. Eighty-seven dead rats in there."

Papa rocks back on his heels. "Any explanation?"

"Rats dying in a wall . . . happens. It's the quantity that bothers me."

Papa sighs. "Could be anything."

"I know it. Keep your eyes open. That's all I'm saying."

"I sleep with them open."

"I'll bet you do."

Before I leave, I check on my patient, Caroline. She's sleeping peacefully, her hair fanning out over the pillow, her arm set on the broken paddle piece. Jing's bandages are rolled neatly around her arm, anchored by her thumb. Not bad for my first broken arm. I only wish Caroline went to

Miss Barstow's. I imagine her telling the other girls. This would impress them, wouldn't it?

I climb into the buggy, badgering Papa with questions. "How was I supposed to know how to set a broken arm and calm a terrified little girl?"

Papa's long legs search for a comfortable spot in the cramped buggy. He has to duck when going through doorways and punch extra holes in the stirrup leathers to make them long enough for his legs. I hope I don't get that tall.

"You figured it out, though, didn't you?"

I can't help smiling. I like being good at this. "Why are you teaching me? Billy was supposed to be the doctor."

"Why are you learning?"

"There are no girls in medical school."

"There are a few." He smiles tenderly, taking a lock of my hair and putting it on the right side of my part. "You did well."

I soak this up.

"Just don't forget that everybody reacts to chloroform differently. Always pay close attention to the small things."

"Are there charts that tell you *exactly* how much by age and by weight?"

"Yes, but don't be a slave to charts. You don't want to be one of those physicians who operate with an open atlas before them."

"I'm to operate now?"

He flashes a boyish smile. "Not this week."

I know what he's saying, but what if I make a mistake? Too much chloroform can kill a person.

"Does Dr. Roumalade have charts?"

Dr. Roumalade is the doctor for people who live on Nob Hill. He makes house calls, like Papa does, but he also has an office, with a room just for people to wait. You have to be a high-muck-a-muck to see Dr. Roumalade. If you're a railroad king and get sick, he'll move in with you until you get well.

"Yes, but I'm certain he uses his eyes and ears more than his charts."

I bet he doesn't get paid in blackberry jam and hand-woven blankets, the way Papa does. It's easier to get your fee if the outcome is good. For his healthy baby boy, Mr. Jessen probably gave Papa a few dollars besides the jam and the blanket, but I don't know for sure. Grown-ups don't give straight answers about money.

"Why is Dr. Roumalade Aunt Hortense's doctor, not you?"

"It would be awkward," Papa says.

"And what was Mr. Jessen talking about, anyway? Eighty-seven rats dying."

"Hygiene is not what it could be in some of our eating establishments."

"But so many!"

"I've got my hands full worrying about human diseases. I can't keep track of rat ailments, too, Lizzie."

After the boat ride through thick wet fog, Jing appears in front of the Ferry Building.

I scurry ahead of Papa and climb up into the buggy behind Jing. "How'd you know what ferry we'd be on?"

"Magic," Jing says, and smiles. His eyebrows move an awful lot. They tell you more than his lips.

The buggy rocks as Papa climbs in. He slides his bags under the seat.

"Does Dr. Roumalade travel as much as you do?" I ask.

"Nope." Papa gives me a dry smile. "He sends inconvenient patients to me."

Jing slaps the lines, and Juliet leaps forward.

"Everything okay at home?" Papa asks as we pass a mule and wagon. *Hee-haw,* the mule warns; we've come too close.

"At home, yes, sir. But Chinatown is under quarantine."

"Chinatown." Papa shakes his head.

I watch up ahead, where a policeman on horseback manages the overflowing line of people waiting for the cable car. "What's the quarantine for?"

"The plague," Papa says.

"The plague? Right, Papa." I laugh.

"It's true. The fact that nobody's seen hide nor hair of it is apparently beside the point. A lot of Sturm und Drang for nothing."

Jing nods, but I don't. What is Sturm und Drang?

"Why is the quarantine happening, then?" I ask.

"Just the word shakes everybody up. Plague victims die a hard death."

"Do they all die?"

"Death rate is fifty percent. Nearly wiped out Europe during the Middle Ages."

"Is it because of the rats?"

"Don't jump to conclusions, Lizzie. You know better than that."

"There must be some reason they think we have the plague."

"There was an outbreak in Hawaii. But there hasn't been a single confirmed case here."

"Why did they quarantine Chinatown?"

"Well . . . they're not going to quarantine Nob Hill, now, are they?" Papa winks at Jing.

Jing smiles.

Aunt Hortense hurries out the second she sees us, like she's been watching through the window. Sometimes she looks so much like Mama, it feels like a twist of the forceps on my heart. But when she opens her mouth, she's Aunt Hortense again. "Thank goodness you're safe," she says.

"Do you think I'd let anything happen to my Lizzie?" Papa asks.

"Promise me you won't take her with you for a while," Aunt Hortense pleads.

"What are you concerned about, Hortense?" My father's voice is patient, as always.

"When was the last time they quarantined a part of the city?"

"I can't recall." Papa climbs down from the buggy after me.

Aunt Hortense fans her face. "My point exactly."

"Is Karl worried?"

"Not a bit. Look, humor me, Jules. I don't want to take chances with our Elizabeth."

Papa nods. "Of course. She'll stay home until this dies down."

"Thanks." Aunt Hortense kisses Papa lightly on the cheek.

"Wait. . . . Papa!" I whisper when we are out of earshot of Aunt Hortense. "We didn't go near the quarantine today, and we're not going tomorrow, either, are we?"

"Nope."

"Then there's no reason for her to be worried. Come on, Papa. What am I going to do at home?"

Papa slips his spectacles off and cleans them with a cloth he keeps in his breast pocket. "Your aunt does a lot for us. If a small thing like this can make her happy . . ."

"But you're the doctor, and you're not worried. Why do we have to listen to her?"

"Because she's your aunt and she loves you."

One word from Aunt Hortense and my whole weekend is ruined. I kick the cobblestones so hard it hurts my toe.

Our Cat's in a Drunken Tizzy

Saturday morning I hear the snap of Papa's bags closing without me. I watch through my window as he hurries across to the barn, hunched forward in the foggy morning, a bag in each hand. A few minutes later, the buggy wheels squeak and Juliet's hooves *click, clack* on the cobblestone.

Great. I'm stuck here all day with nothing to do and no one to do it with.

For a second I wonder what the girls from Miss Barstow's are doing. Then I come to my senses and take out my journal. I like to write poems, just as my mama did. She wrote a poem about me when I was little. It's one of the few things I have from her.

I have a little girl named Lizzie,
So busy she makes me dizzy.

She thinks our pets are ill
And prescribes a doctor's pill.
Now our cat's in a drunken tizzy,
All because of our little Lizzie.

I'm glad Mama had a sense of humor, but I wonder what else she thought about me. Too tall? Too awkward? Too many freckles? Would she be happy that I can saddle my own horse and put together the loose bones in Papa's bone bag to create a skeleton by myself?

Papa says Mama let me do as I pleased more than Aunt Hortense thought she should. Funny how when Mama was alive, I never thought about her. She was like the back of my head—my parietal bone. Always a part of me. Now I wish I'd paid more attention to her.

After she died, Billy and I did everything together. We put on magic shows of tricks Jing taught us. I was his assistant. He tried to saw me in half for the neighbor kids. I had to stay rolled up in an apple crate while he sawed away. Other days, I sawed him. We won two sarsaparillas and a bag of butterscotch candy for that once. He taught me how to ride bareback, how to climb, and how to keep from hurting myself when I jump down from the loft. Now Billy is a grouch who won't even eat supper with us.

He's trying to earn money for a horseless carriage, and that's all he thinks about. I don't know why he wants a stinky old motorcar when he can have a horse.

I watch him test a bike he's repaired. He rides it across the cobblestones, then comes to a skidding halt to check the brakes. He charges a nickel to change a bicycle tire. He will have to change an awful lot of tires to buy an automachine.

I take John Henry out of his stall and begin brushing him.

Billy hops off the bike and leans it against the barn door. "Don't make Aunt Hortense crazy," he says. Last Thanksgiving, Aunt Hortense caught me riding Juliet in my overalls. She was so mad, you'd think I'd robbed a bank. Papa started taking me on his calls after that to get me out of Aunt Hortense's hair.

"I'm just grooming, not riding."

He snorts. "I'm taking him anyway. Why are you here? I thought you'd taken my place as Papa's little helper."

"Aunt Hortense pitched a fit, so Papa said I had to stay home. She thinks I'm going to catch something."

Orange Tom skulks by. He has dirty pumpkin-colored fur, eyes the color of overripe pears, and a paw with an extra finger.

Billy goes into the tack room for the harness.

"Quit following me," he barks.

"I'm not following you. I'm walking in the same direction."

Billy lifts the collar over John Henry's head. He can harness John Henry to the wagon in his sleep. It's harder than it looks. I've tried.

I watch him load the bicycle he fixed into the back of the wagon, climb up, and pick up the lines.

"Where are you going?" I ask.

"Nowhere," he snaps.

"Gosh, Billy, can't you at least tell me that?"

"Nope."

In the house, I unlace my boots, slip them off, and slide in my stocking feet to Papa's library. I kneel on the rug to look at the bottom shelf of journals, searching for articles about interesting diseases. I dream of the day when the girls at Miss Barstow's come down with cholera and I'm the one who saves them.

I look up the plague. The antidotes are wild. Eat snake, wear camphor or dried toads in a locket, fill an amulet with arsenic, keep your farts in a jar, and take an ice water enema. I look up "enema." "The injection of fluid into the rectum." I can't wait to tell Aunt Hortense.

Jing has gone to market; tall, curly-haired Maggy whisks the cobwebs from the ceiling of Papa's library. "Miss Lizzie wishes she could go with Mr. Doctor," Maggy mutters.

"I sure do," I tell her. "What about you, Maggy? What do you wish?"

She doesn't answer. What does Maggy wish for? I have no idea.

There's got to be something better to do than watch Maggy dust. I take the journals up to my room and keep reading. Maybe if I know all about the plague, I can convince Aunt Hortense there's nothing to worry about.

Symptoms, I write. *Fever, swelling in lymph nodes, black-and-blue marks, chills, headaches.*

* * *

When the clock strikes four, Papa, Jing, and Billy are still gone. Papa is often out on calls for days at a time. I don't worry about him. Billy comes home late a lot of nights too. But Jing should be back by now.

I'm reading *The Adventures of Huckleberry Finn* yet again when I hear a noise up on the third floor, where the servants live. Maggy Doyle has a way of being everywhere at once, like a dust storm. Still, I thought she was downstairs.

"Maggy!" I yell.

Not a sound from up above.

Could Papa be back? I would have heard him in the barn. Must be Jing. I jump off the bed and head for the stairs.

Maggy appears in the hall. "Miss Lizzie?"

"Is Jing home?"

"No."

Sometimes houses just creak. Maggy's curly head disappears down the stairway, and I go back to reading in my room. But there it is again—more like shuffling than creaking.

Rats? Mice?

Orange Tom usually takes care of them.

I tiptoe down the hall to the stairway that leads to the servants' floor. The stairs are narrow, dark, and steep, and the stairwell is stuffy.

The door at the top is closed. I turn the crystal handle, and the door swings open.

The third-floor hall looks like the second-floor hall, but there's no furniture, no pictures, and the rug is worn thin. Heat rises, so this floor should be warm, but the windows are wide open. In front of Maggy Doyle's closed door is a mat, as if this is the outside. Jing's door has a paper lantern hanging from the knob.

What if there's a burglar? What if he climbed in the window? With Billy and Papa gone, it's my responsibility to find out. Aunt Hortense wouldn't agree, but since when do I do what she says?

And then a girl whispers: "Lizzie."

The hair on the back of my neck stands up straight. Who is this? I don't know the voice, but this girl knows my name.

I don't believe in ghosts. I watched Papa examine a dead person before. The dead are gone. They can't return.

"Lizzie." It's coming from Jing's room.

"How do you know me?" My voice trembles.

The bevels in the crystal doorknob flicker in the sunlight as the knob turns, making a kaleidoscope pattern on the floor. The door swings open, and a boy stands before me.

The Secret Boy

My knees shake. I open my mouth to scream.

But wait . . . he's just a kid.

He's Chinese, with a square face and a sturdy build. He's a little shorter than me, with straight black hair. He wears a white shirt and a tie. Threads of color hang from his sleeve.

"Who are you?" I try to sound calm.

"I'm Jing's son."

He's lying. "Jing doesn't have a son."

"Yes, he does."

"I would know if Jing had a son. He would have told me."

The boy squints at me as if my answer pains him.

"What? He would have."

He sighs. "You don't know anything," he whispers.

"You can't talk to me that way."

"I'm sorry," he mumbles, though it doesn't seem like he means it.

The way he moves his lips and his eyebrows is shockingly like Jing. Could he be telling the truth? Is he Jing's son?

"What's your name?"

"Noah."

"How old are you?"

"Twelve."

"What are you doing in my house?"

"I live here."

"Live *here*?"

"I do now. In here."

I survey the room, which is clean and smells of almonds and cooked rice. A cot with a red silk quilt rests against one wall; a large dragon tapestry hangs from another. An unlit candle and blue-and-white ceramic bowls sit on a bookshelf full of books.

"Where do you sleep?"

Noah lifts up the quilt and pulls a white pad from under the bed. I go inside to see.

"I thought you were a girl," I say.

"Well, I'm not," he shoots back.

"Does anyone know you live here?"

He shakes his head.

Maggy's room is next door. "Not even Maggy?"

"No."

"Why are you living here in secret?"

He sucks his lips in. "I'm not a servant," he whispers.

I try to think if I have known any Chinese who are not servants. The vegetable peddler? The men who work at the cleaners?

"Do you go to school?"

He nods.

"The Chinese school?" I saw the Chinese school once. The kids wore silk skullcaps and silk trousers. He's not dressed that way.

"Yes."

I kneel down and run my finger along the spines of one shelf of books. *The Brothers Karamazov, Around the World in Eighty Days, The Origin of Species.* Is Noah reading these?

"I also do piecework. Five cents a dozen." He picks up a stack of buttonhole strips, which explains the colored threads hanging from his sleeve. They are needles with thread. "Baba doesn't want me to get used to waiting on people."

"Who is Baba?"

"Jing. *'Baba'* is 'Papa' in Chinese."

He gets to call Jing "Baba"? "Why doesn't he want you to wait on people? *He* waits on people."

"Yes, but he says it makes you invisible."

"Jing, invisible? Never!" I stare at him. "Are you crazy?"

His eyes go cross-eyed and he sticks his fingers into his mouth to stretch it out like a weird jack-o'-lantern. "Do I look crazy?"

I shake my head; I can't help smiling.

He bites at his lip. "Baba should be back by now."

He's right. Going to market takes a few hours, not all day.

"Do you know where he is?" I ask.

"I'm afraid they caught him."

"Caught him? Who? What are you talking about?"

"The police."

I sit back on my heels. "Why would the police want Jing?"

"The quarantine." He walks to the window and pulls the blind back just enough to peek out. "They want us all in Chinatown."

"Jing lives here with us. Not in Chinatown. He always has."

"That doesn't matter."

"Of course it matters."

"You know so little," he whispers.

"I know *a lot*!"

"Miss Lizzie?" Maggy calls from the distant downstairs.

Noah takes a step closer. "Wait. Will you find out where he is?"

"Me? How am I going to—"

"Miss Lizzie!" Maggy opens and closes the doors on the second floor as if she thinks I might be hiding in a closet.

"And promise you won't tell anyone I'm here," he pleads.

First he insults me. Now . . . Who is this kid anyway?

"They'll fire him if you do."

Jing has worked for us since I was three. He has made every one of my birthday cakes for as long as I can remember. He bakes a surprise in each one—chocolate filling, strawberries, licorice, peppermint candies. Each year I look forward to what he's baked inside. He makes me lemonade on hot days and hot cocoa on cold ones. He cuts me big slabs of bread warm from the oven and slathered with honey. Once, when I sprained my ankle, he read me all of *Sara Crewe, or What Happened at Miss Minchin's* while I sat with my leg propped up on pillows.

When I come home from Miss Barstow's, where I have sat by myself, worked by myself, read by myself, it's Jing who makes me laugh with his imitation of a market merchant trying to sell a pigeon as a goose, or the iceman's horse who has a crush on Juliet.

"No one will fire Jing."

"They will." Noah's whisper is strained.

"Never!" I say, but . . . Aunt Hortense and Uncle Karl own our house. They won't be happy about a boy who doesn't work for us living here in secret.

I nod. "I'll keep quiet . . . until Papa comes home."

CHAPTER 6

Second Helpings

The upstairs is so silent, it seems impossible that a boy is up there. Did I imagine him? How long has he been here? Where is his mother? How does he sneak in and out for school?

I sit on my bed, looking out at the sky, which is dark gray, lit orange at the horizon. The yard is a hazy pink. I turn on the electric light, which is unreliable. Uncle Karl says soon we will use only electric lights. I hope not, because the gaslights work much better.

Why would Noah say he's not going to be a servant? Doesn't he understand the way things are? And where is Jing, anyway?

"Miss Lizzie!" Maggy breezes through, the bright green parrot on her shoulder, my mended bloomers in her hand. She smiles at me. "Supper's ready."

"Supper's ready! Supper's ready!" Mr. P. squawks.

My stomach grumbles. Supper without Jing will be dull indeed. Wait. What about Noah? How will he get supper?

In the kitchen, Maggy has warmed Jing's beef stew and ladled it into a bowl. She has cut Jing's bread and spread butter on it for me.

"Where's Jing?" I ask.

"At the market." Maggy sets the bowl at my place.

"It's too late for that."

Maggy doesn't answer. She knows that if Jing is not here, she must warm supper. Does she think beyond that?

Sunday afternoon is Jing's time off. Sometimes he doesn't return until late in the night, but today is Saturday. He never takes Saturday off.

When Maggy heads for the drawing room to get the skeins of ribbons she fashions into bows for my hair, I return what's left of my stew to the pot. Then I slip back into my seat and ask for seconds.

She ladles more hot stew into the bowl and spreads another slice of bread with butter.

"I'm going to eat this upstairs," I tell her.

She looks up from where she stands at the counter, black grosgrain ribbon wound around her fingers. "Miss Lizzie sick?"

"I just want to eat in my room."

She gets a tray for the soup and bread, pours a full glass of milk, and then carries the tray up the stairs and sets it on the bed without spilling a drop. Maggy would do anything in the world I asked. Once, she stayed up for three nights to finish the smocking on a pinafore for me.

"Thank you." I beam at her.

I listen for her footsteps down the stairs, the swing of the door, and the squeak of her stool. Then I pick up the tray and head for the servants' stairs, aware of each step and how it rocks the milk.

Outside Jing's door, my heart beats loudly. "Noah?" I whisper.

Noah cracks open the door. His eyes shift back and forth. He looks down at the tray. "You brought supper?"

I nod.

He moves out of the way, and I slip inside.

Where do I set the tray? I almost laugh, thinking about asking Miss Barstow this question, given all the rules I'm breaking. Entering a boy's room, not announcing yourself with a calling card, serving a servant.

Noah sees me hesitate. He takes the tray and sets it on the silk blanket. I'm not as steady with the tray as Maggy. A little of the milk has spilled.

Noah's eyes are hungry, but he takes a step back, offering the stew to me.

"I've eaten." I spot a chair piled high with books. Noah clears the chair, and I sit down.

He climbs back into the nest of books and button strips on his bed and tucks into his stew, nibbling at his bread as if he wants it to last. He has a habit of pushing his hair behind his ears after every few bites.

"One thing I don't understand. . . . Why did Jing go to Chinatown?"

"He's a translator."

"What does he translate?"

Noah looks at me like I'm an idiot. "Chinese to English."

"Of course." I turn red. "Papa isn't home. I don't know if he'll be back tonight. I'm going to talk to Uncle Karl. If Jing got caught in the quarantine, Uncle Karl will get him out."

"How?"

"Uncle Karl is in the newspaper business. He owns the evening *Call* and S&S Sugar. People like to be on his good side."

Noah stops chewing. His eyes watch me warily. "Are you going to tell him about me?"

I shake my head. "No."

He lets out an uneasy breath. "Baba will be mad I told you."

"Jing never gets mad."

Noah laughs.

"What? He doesn't."

"Not with you," he whispers. "He works for you."

Is this true? Is there another Jing I don't know about? "What does Jing say about me?"

Noah thinks about this. "He trusts you. He says you're kind to Maggy Doyle, but . . . you're your own worst enemy."

What? I'm my own worst enemy? "Why does he say that?"

Noah shrugs. "But he loves you. I thought you'd be the person I could trust."

"Not Billy?"

"Baba thinks Billy has lost his way."

"He has not," I say. I don't want this strange boy talking about my brother. I stare hard at Noah. How can he know so much about us?

Downstairs, I'm putting on my boots to go talk to Uncle Karl when I remember that it's Jing's job to feed the animals. The horses are both gone—Juliet with Papa, John Henry with Billy. Orange Tom feeds himself. Maggy feeds the parrot, but the chickens . . .

"The chickens need to be fed," I tell Maggy.

Maggy scrambles for her coat. She picks up a lantern—no electricity in the barn—and the basket of stale bread. I follow her outside, where the moon is a lopsided circle, a bird hoots like an owl, and the dark shapes of the hedges create spooky moon shadows. Maggy shines the lantern on the path.

The path is as familiar to me as my own feet, but it seems different tonight. I glance up at Noah's window. Is he watching me?

I leave Maggy tossing stale bread in the coop and walk up the path to the Sweeting house, all four floors lit brightly.

When I go in, maids in black uniforms are just removing the supper dishes from the long dining room table. The way they're talking and laughing, I know Aunt Hortense isn't nearby. When the maids spy me, the giggling comes to an abrupt halt.

Uncle Karl is in the smoking room, a brandy snifter in his hand. He's deep in conversation with a man who has a half-moon of black curly hair circling his shiny balding head. I'm not allowed in the leather-walled smoking room—no girls are, not even Aunt Hortense. I wait for a break in the conversation.

"Hearst put it on the front page," the man says.

Uncle Karl groans. "Only Hearst would sanction this ridiculous escapade."

"The plague sells papers. They're flying off the stands," the balding man says.

"It's bad for the city. We've all agreed. Can't someone get Hearst on board?" Uncle Karl asks.

"Good luck with that." The balding man steadies his glass as Uncle Karl fills it from a crystal carafe. "You don't suppose any of this is true, do you?"

"There isn't a doctor in the state who believes it is."

"Still. If it were, the prospect is . . ."

"Unthinkable. But I don't build my business on speculation, any more than you do. You got something you're not telling me?"

"Nope." The man clinks his glass with Uncle Karl's.

"Then we'll leave the scaremongering to Hearst. It will backfire soon enough. It always does."

They're silent.

"Uncle Karl?" I call from the doorway.

"Excuse me, will you?" Uncle Karl appears out of the smoke. "Why, Lizzie." He takes a puff of his cigar. "To what do I owe this pleasure?"

Uncle Karl's jackets fit better than Papa's or Billy's. Aunt Hortense says there is only one tailor in the city who is skilled enough to suit him. No matter the time of day, Uncle Karl is freshly pressed, as if he just stepped into his clothes. He has gray hair, and a kind face with sharp blue eyes. Aunt Hortense is taller than he is.

"Jing is gone. He went to the market this morning, and he hasn't come back. I'm worried he got caught in the quarantine."

"The quarantine? Darlin', you shouldn't worry your pretty little head about such things."

I can't help smiling at this. No one says I'm pretty except Uncle Karl. "But what about Jing?"

Uncle Karl clicks his tongue. "He's a grown man. There's no telling where he is."

"He wouldn't go off without telling us. It's not like him. He must be in the quarantine." I wish I could tell Uncle Karl that Jing's son is certain Jing is there.

Uncle Karl holds his cigar and his glass with his left hand. With his right, he slides his gold pocket watch out of his vest pocket and glances at it. "It's possible," he concedes. "I'll make some calls tomorrow and see what I can find out, but only for you, Peanut." He winks at me.

"What about tonight?"

He swirls the brandy in his glass. "What can I do at nine o'clock at night? I'll look into it first thing in the morning."

"Yes, sir," I say. "Thank you."

"Is Billy home?"

"I'm not sure," I mumble.

His sharp eyes cut through me. "You're not sure, or you don't want to say?"

I waggle my head back and forth. "A little of both, sir."

"I wish your father would let me buy Billy a motorcar. Then your brother wouldn't be out trying to make money every hour of the day and night."

"Papa wants him to earn it himself."

"I know he does. Your father is a noble man, but the world is not nearly as noble as he is, Peanut, and don't you forget it."

"Papa wouldn't agree with you about that, sir."

"No, I expect not."

What would my father say about all of this? I stop to think. "He'd say it's up to us to shape the world. And not the other way around."

"And what do you think, Peanut?"

"I think Papa's way is nicer."

"Hah, yes." He chuckles. "It most certainly is, darlin'. It most certainly is."

Chocolate Brussels Sprouts

I walk back to my house, the wind blowing the fog like ghosts chasing through the streets. No light in Noah's window. Is there enough light coming under the door for him to read, or does he have to go to bed when the sun goes down?

Maggy's light is on. Too bad. I want to run up and tell Noah that Uncle Karl said he'd help. I miss having another kid in the house. I wish for the thousandth time that Billy would be like he used to be.

As soon as I wake up, I run to Papa's room, but his coat is not hanging from the knob, his pocket watch and loose change are not on the dresser. His bed is untouched.

Billy's door is closed. When I was little, we used to sneak out to ride before Aunt Hortense got up. Now I don't dare knock on his door. He'll tear my head off if I wake him.

Downstairs, I hear the familiar sound of coal being shoveled. Jing! I run out the door and around to the cellar stairs. The door is open, but Maggy is shoveling, her curly hair pinned to her head, a streak of soot on her cheek and perspiration marks under her arms. She smiles up at me.

"Jing is still gone?"

She nods. I run out to the barn to see if John Henry is back. If he's here, Billy is, too.

John Henry stands with his lower lip so loose, you could collect pennies in it. I slip into his stall and put my arms around his fuzzy brown-and-white neck. I open a bale of hay and toss him a flake. He plods over to his manger and roots around. When his head pops up, his forelock is laced with alfalfa.

Usually on Sundays, Billy, Papa, Aunt Hortense, and I go to church. Uncle Karl doesn't like church. He says, *Going to church doesn't make a person a Christian any more than taking a mule into a barn makes the mule a horse.* He rides out to Ocean Beach or down to the racetrack to get stories for his newspaper column.

Last night he said he'd find out about Jing first thing. But Uncle Karl's first thing could be a week from tomorrow. Still, this is an emergency. He knows that, doesn't he?

In the kitchen, Maggy has made oatmeal, but everything she cooks tastes like boiled potatoes.

It's messy to carry a bowl of hot cereal up two flights

of stairs and then bring the dirty bowl back down. I fill a pitcher of water, then make two apple butter sandwiches, grab a jar of peaches and two forks, and roll everything into a kitchen towel. Noah won't like Maggy's boiled-potato oatmeal any better than I do.

While Maggy is in the chicken coop gathering eggs, I run up to the third floor.

"Noah," I whisper, knocking softly.

No one answers.

I knock again.

Still nothing. Is he asleep?

If I knock too loudly, Billy might hear. But I can't just leave Noah's breakfast outside his door. How would I explain that to Maggy?

What am I supposed to do in a situation like this? Again I think of Miss Barstow's etiquette rules.

"Noah," I whisper, opening the door.

Inside, the room is still. The dragon wall tapestry. The black lacquer table. The pitcher and washbasin. The red silken bedcover. The books.

"Noah," I whisper, a little more loudly this time.

Tlick-tick. The closet door opens. Noah ducks out from under the shirts, hopping over a kerosene lantern.

A flicker of joy flashes in his eyes, and then he scowls. "This is my room! You can't just barge in anytime you want."

It's not his room. Uncle Karl and Aunt Hortense own our house.

"Well . . . I was bringing you breakfast."

"You scared me." He chews on his lip. "I heard footsteps."

"We need a way for me to know it's okay to come in. I can't be knocking."

"No," he agrees. "We could hang something on the door."

"Maggy might notice. What would she think about things appearing on Jing's door when Jing isn't here?"

"How about the window? If we drape something small over the blind? Would she notice that?"

"Probably not."

He opens the closet, stands on his tiptoes, and runs his hand along the high shelf. Dust motes fill the air; a ball of red yarn falls down. He pulls out a gold braided cord with a tassel on each end.

"That's good," I say, "but what if it's not safe to come up? Is there a way to get a message to you?"

Noah's eyes rove the room. "Orange Tom comes up here. We can attach messages to his collar."

"What if someone finds the message? What if they read it?"

"We'll have to be careful what we write," he says as I unroll the kitchen towel and take out the apple butter sandwiches and the jar of peaches. He spreads a cloth on his bed, as if we are having a picnic, and I set the sandwiches on it, open the peaches, and hand him a fork.

His eyes widen. "You're going to eat with me?"

"Sure," I say. I don't want him to know I've never eaten with Jing or Maggy before.

I take a bite of my sandwich. Noah tries to stab a peach with his fork.

"I talked to Uncle Karl. He said he'd help."

Some of the stiffness in Noah's shoulders melts away. He stares at the door as if Jing will come through at any minute.

Is it mean to tell him that it may be a while? Papa says never give a patient more information than he can handle.

"In Chinatown, do you live with your mother?"

"Mama's in China. I live with my uncle Han."

At the wharf, I've seen people coming off the steamships from the Orient. Women in bright Chinese clothes, men in black derbies and baggy pants carrying lacquer chests, spices, bamboo, bolts of fabric, large jade figurines, teak furniture. Everyone comes here. Does anyone return?

"She went back to China?"

"She never came over. It's hard for women to leave."

"I'm sorry," I say. "Do you write her?"

"No."

"Why not?" If I could write my mother, I certainly would.

He shrugs, then takes a bite of sandwich. I wait for him to say more. Finally I offer, "My mama is gone, too."

He nods. "Baba talks about her sometimes."

"He does? What does he say?"

Noah's mouth bunches to one side. "She was kind. She hired him even though he'd never been a cook before."

My mother was kind. It feels good to hear this. Papa doesn't talk about Mama. He misses her too much.

"She liked to play practical jokes, and she loved chocolate. Chocolate cookies, chocolate ice cream . . . She even had chocolate sauce on broccoli once."

"Chocolate broccoli," I say, laughing. "And chocolate-covered brussels sprouts, too."

"It was your mama's idea for him to bake things in your birthday cake."

"Really?"

He nods.

Mama celebrates my birthday with me. Am I just like the Lizzie I was when I was little? Would she love me now, the way she did then?

"Baba said she adored you, and when she realized she was going to die, she made him promise to stay until you grew up."

My mouth drops open. "What?" It never occurred to me that Jing would ever leave. Family members can't decide they won't be family anymore. But of course, Jing is not family. He's staying because he promised Mama.

Noah nods.

I look around Jing's room. The walls are the same as the walls in my room. The floor. The doorframe. The closet. But the room is filled with foreign things.

"Why are you here?" I ask Noah. "You came before the quarantine, didn't you?"

"We heard that it might happen. Baba wanted me out."

"He was worried about the plague?"

"He was worried I'd starve."

"Starve!"

"Everything is closed off. Nothing is allowed in. A lot of people think it's a way to get rid of us."

"Who wants to get rid of you?"

"People like you."

"*Me?* I don't want to get rid of you. I just brought you food."

"Not you."

Who would want Jing to starve? Jing has made almost every meal I've ever eaten. There was always enough. I couldn't stand it if Jing were hungry.

Noah stops chewing. "What's the matter?"

Papa says you shouldn't lie to a patient, but you needn't add to their worries by piling on your own. "I'm worried about Jing, too."

He sinks his teeth into his sandwich. "My name in Chinese is Choy, which means 'wealthy.' When I grow up, I'm going to own a bank with lots of money and free food."

"Shall I call you Choy?"

"You should call me by my American name."

I nod. "How are you going to get the money for your bank?"

"I'm thinking on that. Maybe I'll learn in college."

He's going to college? I can't even go to college. "Do Chinese people go to college?"

"Some," he says.

"Some women go to college, too."

He snorts. "Don't tell me you want to."

"I do." I've never said it out loud before.

His brow furrows. "It'll be hard."

"You think I'm stupid?"

"You're not as smart as I am."

"What? That's not a nice thing to say. How would you know, anyway?"

"You're a girl. You'll get married, like all girls do."

"I'm not getting married." The flush rises in my cheeks. "Wives have to do what they're told."

"Maybe you could marry a stupid husband, and then you could make all the decisions."

I frown. "What would I do with a stupid husband?"

"If you got tired of him, you could take him to an auction."

"A stupid-husband auction?" I ask. "Would the amount of money you got for him be based on how stupid he was?"

"Yes, so you'd have to prove his stupidity," Noah says.

"My husband is so stupid . . . he fills the saltshaker through the little holes in the top."

Noah grins. "Maybe you are smart enough for college. I'll help you if it's too hard."

"I'll help *you* if it's too hard."

He laughs, then screws the top onto the jar of peaches and hands it back.

"Keep it. In case you get hungry later."

He frowns at me. "Okay, but . . . I just want you to know, I don't have girls for friends."

"Why not?"

"Girls lie."

"They *do not*! Well, maybe some, but not me. Why would you say that?"

"In Chinatown there's a girl who lies."

"That's just one. Not every girl lies."

"I suppose not." His eyes search my face. "Are you telling me everything you know about Baba?"

I meet his gaze squarely. I want this boy to like me. I hope he can't see just how much. But doesn't he have to like me, because I'm white and he's Chinese? "I don't know anything."

He wraps a thread around his thumb so tightly, the flesh bunches out in little puckers. "Your uncle Karl said he'd find out."

"I know. He will!"

"But you're not sure," he finishes for me.

"He said he would," I whisper. "I just don't know when exactly."

Noah weaves the thread around the rest of his fingers, and then pulls tight. "You could be my friend"—his eyes are on his fingers—"if you tell me a secret about you."

"And you'll tell me a secret about you?"

"You already know one about me."

I lean forward. "I want another."

"You first."

I take a big gulping breath. "I don't have any friends," I whisper.

"Why not?"

"I don't know. I'm just . . . different. I don't like what they like, and the second I open my mouth, I stick my foot into it."

It feels good to let this out.

He sighs as if he knows what this is like. "Is that all? Because that's nothing. We can figure that out."

"How?"

He smiles his crazy smile. "Is there one girl you like better than the rest?"

"Not really."

"There is. There always is."

"Well, maybe," I admit.

"Next time you go to school, look around. You'll see which one she is. Start with her."

I nod. "Okay. Now you."

"In Chinatown there are six companies that run the place. And there are six of us boys who lead the kids. If you ever need anything from a kid in Chinatown, say you're a friend of Six of Six."

"Fine, but not that kind of secret. Something personal."

"Oh, you mean a girl secret. I don't have girl secrets."

"I told *you* a girl secret."

"Of course you did. You're a girl. Mine was better. Mine was useful."

I laugh. "Come on. You have one. I know you do."

"Okay." He leans in and whispers, "I don't know how to throw up."

"What? Everyone knows how to throw up."

He shakes he head. "Nope. Never done it. Don't know how."

"You want me to give you lessons?" I ask.

We laugh. Pretty soon I'm demonstrating and we're

giggling so hard, we've got our hands over each other's mouths to keep quiet.

I stand up. I've been on the third floor a long time. I don't want anyone coming to look for me.

"Tell me the second you hear from Uncle Karl, okay?" Noah whispers as I tiptoe into the hall. "And, Lizzie . . . come back as soon as you can."

Mama's Daughter

After church, I hover outside Billy's door. Why is he still asleep? He'll be crabby if I wake him, but I need his help.

When I knock, he barks, "What?"

"Can I come in?"

"I'm sleeping."

I crack open the door. He grabs his extra pillow and pulls it over his head.

"Billy, I need you."

"For what?" His voice is muffled.

"To take me to Chinatown. We have to find Jing."

"Why?"

"He's caught in the quarantine. If we tell them he's our cook and he doesn't live in Chinatown, maybe they'll let him come home."

"You're making this up."

I pluck the pillow off his head. A purplish-red half-moon rings his left eye. His lower lid is red and swollen. The white of his eye is pink.

"What happened to your eye?"

His hand covers his face. "Ran into a doorframe," he mumbles.

I pull his hand away and gently inspect his face.

"Where?"

"Where what?"

"Was the door?"

"Don't ask so many questions."

"It's only one. This doesn't look like it needs sutures. Put some ice on it," I advise.

"I'm not going to take you."

"But what about Jing?"

He pulls the pillow back over his face. "What about him? Look, I've got things to do. Now get out of here."

Outside his room, I cross my arms and stare down the door. Jing taught Billy how to juggle, ride a bike, and make coins appear out of thin air. Jing played hide-and-seek with us in the barn every night before bed. Jing saved us the butter-frosting bowl even when Papa said it wasn't good for our teeth. Doesn't Billy care about Jing at all?

I'm going to find Jing. Mama would want me to. I know she would.

The wagon is hard to hook up. Should I ride? I'm a good rider, but I don't like sidesaddles, and there's no telling what Aunt Hortense will do if she catches me riding bareback again.

It takes me the better part of an hour to get the harness on John Henry and the wagon attached the right way. It's a foggy, gray day, but my hair is pasted down with sweat and my jacket is glued to my back when I'm finished. Still, I'm proud of myself. No other girl at Miss Barstow's would be able to lift the collar or attach the traces, much less drive a wagon or go to Chinatown. This feeling lasts for a minute and a half, before I realize that John Henry has to pull the wagon right by Aunt Hortense's house. What if she hears me? What if I run into someone who will tell her? What if a policeman sees me? It's not against the law for a girl to drive a wagon by herself, but it is unusual.

And how will I get Jing out? I should wait for Papa to come home or for Uncle Karl to help. But who knows when Papa will be back, and how much does Jing matter to Uncle Karl?

I take a deep breath. If I can give a little girl chloroform and set her broken arm, surely I can drive a wagon in broad daylight on a Sunday. I'll stay on the back streets. No one will see me.

Then, too, I've never actually driven before, but I've sat next to Billy and Papa a million times. I know how it's done.

I climb up onto the wagon and give the whip a tentative snap. I don't want to hurt John Henry. He doesn't move. I pop it harder. . . . Nothing. I brandish it in the air and snap it back down with a fierce crack, and the big pinto plods forward, pulling the wagon onto the cobblestones. I keep the whip cracking as we approach the Sweetings' mansion, glancing back at our house. Can Noah see me? I hope so.

It's unusually quiet at the Sweetings'. I'm pretty sure Nettie, Aunt Hortense's head maid, has a staff meeting in the second kitchen right now. That must be where everyone is.

What perfect timing!

I have a big grin on my face when the huge front door opens and Aunt Hortense hurries down the marble steps. "Elizabeth! What in the name of . . ."

Oh no! Gallop, John Henry! I lean forward, ready to take off. But Aunt Hortense will send a servant after me. They'll catch us, and I'll be in even more trouble.

I pull up at the gate.

"What in the world do you think you're doing?" Aunt Hortense is standing on the garden path in her stockinged feet, no hat on her head.

The butler appears behind her carrying her jeweled handbag, boots, and gloves.

There isn't a lie big enough to cover this.

"*You* harnessed John Henry?"

I can't keep the smile off my face.

"Pleased with yourself, are you?"

I try hard not to nod.

"Lizzie!" Billy hurries across the driveway, one boot on, one boot off. "You were supposed to wait in the barn."

My mouth pops open.

"William!" Aunt Hortense stares him down. "She's going with you?"

Billy nods, then cocks his head as if he and Aunt Hortense are in cahoots. "Of course. You know how impatient she is."

Aunt Hortense fans her face with her hand. "I most certainly do."

"I told her I'd take her to the Emporium," Billy rattles on. "Can't you ever follow directions?" he says to me.

"William." Aunt Hortense walks closer. "What happened to your eye?"

"Ran into a doorframe."

"Taller than you thought you were, are you?" Aunt Hortense asks.

"I guess so." Billy smiles his charming smile, but it doesn't do the trick. Not with the one red-rimmed misshapen eye.

"Uncle Karl knows about your eye?" she asks him.

"Yes, ma'am," he says as I scoot over so he can hop in.

"Elizabeth, I won't put up with these kinds of shenanigans. You aren't a little girl anymore. You're to behave like a young woman. When William says to wait in the barn, you are to do as you're told. Should this happen again, I will insist that you board at Miss Barstow's or somewhere else that you will like *even less.* Is that clear?" She glowers at me.

What's worse than boarding at Miss Barstow's? Prison? Billy nudges me with his elbow, and I hold my tongue.

"She's sorry, Aunt Hortense," Billy says.

"Yes, I'm sorry," I say, as stiff as party petticoats.

"You'd better be." Aunt Hortense heads back to her house on tender feet, the butler trailing behind her. Billy slaps John Henry with the lines, and the big horse leaps forward. Billy doesn't need the whip.

"Changed your mind?" I whisper.

Billy sighs. "I miss Jing's banana pancakes."

"That all?"

"Of course not. How do you know Jing's in Chinatown, anyway?"

A bareback rider gallops past us. Stones and dust rise in his wake. "Where else would he be?"

CHAPTER 9
Quarantine

"We would have heard if something happened to him," Billy says. "And the police aren't going to let anyone out of the quarantine lines."

"The *police*?"

"Who do you think is enforcing the quarantine?"

I say nothing as we *clip-clop* by the weird pharmacy where a coiled rattler sleeps in the window. They sell glass eyes and hook hands, besides all the medicines, which claim to remedy every problem you've ever had. Papa says most of them are nothing more than sugar water.

"So, what exactly is your plan?" Billy steers the wagon around a horseless carriage stuck in the road.

"I'm going to tell them he doesn't live in Chinatown, he lives with us. He doesn't belong in the quarantined area. Papa's a doctor. He needs Jing's help."

"We should mention Uncle Karl," Billy says.

"I wish Papa were here. He'd know what to do."

Billy snorts. "I don't."

Papa wants Billy to go to medical school, and he won't take no for an answer. Every time Billy says he might want to do something else, Papa looks like he's getting surgery without anesthesia.

Papa doesn't expect much of me, so he's often pleasantly surprised. That's one good thing about being a girl.

"Why are you so mad at Papa all the time?" I ask.

"I'm not mad at him; he's mad at me. Everything I do disappoints him."

"You used to be nicer."

"You didn't used to be such a Goody Two-shoes."

"I'm not!"

"Oh, Papa, can you show me how to clean a bedsore?" He makes his voice gooey and high-pitched.

"I don't sound like that."

"Yes, you do."

"Well, I'd rather go with him than go to school."

"Still having trouble with those girls?"

I don't answer. We pass two men in matching outfits riding a bicycle built for two.

"You try too hard. That's your problem. They can smell it on you."

How do you try not to try? Or try in a way so that people don't think you're trying? Why can't people just say what they want and be who they are?

"Hey, Billy!" A boy, maybe seventeen, with a plaid cap

and red cheeks waves to him from the back of a wagon. "You sure got a thumping last night."

Billy shrugs as a distant boat toots its horn. "Going to make my two bits back tonight, Oofty. You watch," Billy tells him.

"You're *fighting*? Does Papa know?" I ask.

"Not unless you tell him, you little squealer."

"I'm not a squealer. You know I'm not," I say as a wagon loaded with wood turns down a side street. A few blocks later we pass Dr. Jenkins's Museum, where the head of the world's greatest bandit can be seen in a bottle.

Soon the air begins to smell like burning rubbish. Black pots placed every few yards spew stinking smoke. Wooden sawhorses and ropes circle the haphazard crowded-together buildings of Chinatown. Chinese signs, Chinese characters, Chinese lanterns, and foreign scrollwork—Chinatown is its own city in the middle of our city.

The police in their navy coats and hard bell-shaped helmets are out. I count five on horseback, seven on foot.

Inside the ropes of Chinatown, crowds of Chinese wait for . . . what? Most men have long braids and wear baggy silk clothes. Some are in black with black derbies, some have on bright colors. The few women wear fine embroidered robes and trousers. Some men smoke. Some pace the ropes that cordon off Chinatown.

I scan the crowd. Only a few men are in regular clothes, and none are Jing. I notice the donkey-pulled hearse. When rich men die in San Francisco, they get a carriage drawn by six white horses. When poor men die, they get a wheelbarrow ride or the donkey-pulled hearse. When it passes us, I see that it's empty.

A few minutes later a wagon full of barrels roll by. Strangely, the police let that one out of the quarantine area.

"How did they decide where to rope off?"

"Everything that's Chinese, they quarantined."

"They think white people can't get sick?"

Billy shrugs.

"Papa would be mad if he saw how they're locked in," I say.

"Papa doesn't know half of what happens in this city."

"Let's get closer. Then we can ask about Jing. What's his last name, anyway?"

Billy shakes his head. "Maybe Jing is his last name."

"We don't even know," I whisper. Noah's words flash in my mind. *You don't know anything.*

Billy maneuvers the wagon closer to the quarantine line, away from the cluster of police. "Hey!" I call to a little boy in a red silk jacket. "Do you know if Jing is in there?"

The little boy hops on one foot, then the other. "Jing?" he asks.

"He's our cook."

The boy hops closer. A man in a black derby scolds him, and the little boy scurries away. The other men inside the rope stay away from the boundary. They ignore our calls.

A policeman on foot half-runs toward me. "Move it on!"

"Mr. Policeman, sir." My heart pounds in my chest. "Our cook lives with us. He got caught in the quarantine by accident. Could we get him out?"

"No one's to go in. No one's to go out."

"Yes, but this was a mistake, sir. Our uncle Karl Sweeting is going to be talking to you about it."

The policeman stops. "Mr. Sweeting? He's your uncle?" He peers at us. "I don't know nothing about that. My orders is to keep folks out of here."

"Yes, sir." Billy turns John Henry around.

We walk around the quarantine—far enough away that the police don't bother us. Down a side street we pass officers drinking coffee. I listen in as we roll by.

"You know anything?" a policeman with a red beard asks.

"When it's going to end, you mean?" the officer with his helmet off replies.

"Waiting on the monkey," the third officer replies.

The second officer laughs. "The monkey, is it? City of fools, if you ask me."

"What monkey? What are they talking about?" I whisper to Billy.

"Who knows? It could be a code, or a nickname. There's a man named Monkey Warren."

"But why would this monkey man have anything to do with Chinatown?"

"It's just talk." Billy peers down the block to the barricade. "We're not going to get any closer than this."

In the distance I see a painted dragon and large blue-and-white porcelain vases outside a shop on a deserted street. A man with a pole over his shoulders carries loaded baskets on each end.

Billy circles John Henry back. "We tried, Lizzie."

"We can't leave. Jing's in there."

"Maybe Jing has a lady friend. Maybe he's in Berkeley visiting his cousin. Maybe he told Papa he'd be gone and didn't tell us. Why are you so sure he's in the quarantine?"

John Henry is moving faster. He knows we're headed home. I guess that's one good thing about a motorcar. They don't get barn sour.

"It just makes sense," I say.

"If you're going to be a scientist, you're going to need to prove what you think."

"I know!"

"Look." Billy's eyes are kind now. "Stop worrying about Jing, okay? He'll be back."

I've lost the battle. Billy's going home. If only I knew these policemen the way Uncle Karl does. Wait. Do I know any policemen? That girl Caroline, whose arm I set. Wasn't her father a policeman?

"Billy, wait here for me." I dive from the wagon seat.

"Lizzie! No! LIZZIE!" Billy shouts. I'm holding my skirts up, running fast, jigging and jagging around a spittoon, a tethered horse, a watering trough, and a mounting block.

But when I turn the corner, where the policemen were drinking coffee, they're gone. I keep running toward Chinatown.

The first policeman I see is on horseback, walking the roped-off line.

"Excuse me, sir. Sir!" I wave to him.

"What are you doing out here, young lady?"

"Do you know where Officer Jessen might be?"

The policeman's horse is fidgety. He roots his head. "Jessen? He family of yours?"

"No, sir. He's a friend of my papa's. But it's important. I need to see him."

The policeman nods. "Stay put. I'll get him." His skittery horse leaps forward. I glance back, wondering if Billy will wait, go home, or come find me.

Inside the barricade, I see a policeman start a bonfire in the street; trash and bedding explode in flames.

Thick orange clouds of stinking chemicals rise. People cough, cover their faces with their shirts. Scatter in all directions. A ring of policemen surrounds the fire. Buckets of water appear. Sparks die down with a hiss, then turn to smoke.

Outside the barricade, a big policeman lumbers toward me. Caroline's father.

"Officer Jessen!" I say.

He looks me up and down. "You're Dr. Kennedy's daughter. Aren't you the one who helped my little girl with her arm?"

"Yes, sir. I'm Lizzie."

Out of the corner of my eye, I see Billy driving John Henry down the street toward us. He's driving standing up and motioning for me to come.

"What's the problem, Lizzie?" Officer Jessen asks. "What can I do to help?"

"Our cook, Jing, is in the quarantine. We need to get him out."

Officer Jessen shakes his big head. "If he's in there, I can't get him out."

"But he doesn't belong in Chinatown. He lives with us."

"That isn't the point. If he's in the quarantine area, he's been exposed. If we bring him out here, he could get you sick. Do you understand?"

"Papa says the plague isn't here. He says this is all just—"

"That's not for us to decide, Lizzie. You and I don't make the rules, but we surely must live by them. Now, how'd you get here? Do you need a ride home?"

I point to the wagon. "My brother."

He nods. "You climb up onto that wagon with your brother and you go on home. If this weren't my job, I'd be nowhere near this place, believe me."

"But—"

"I can't help you with this. Now I need you to go on home, you hear?"

I look back at the barricade. On the Chinatown side, a man is running back and forth along the ropes like a caged animal. One policeman shouts at him to stop. Another walks the barrier with a billy club.

A quarantine is to keep infectious diseases from spreading. But there are no doctors or nurses here. No one wears masks or gloves. There is no soap or water. Whatever this is, it's not quarantine for disease at all.

Orange Tom

When we get home, the Sweetings' uniformed houseboys are carrying Aunt Hortense's white antique writing desk, her chair, her steamer trunk, her footbath, her quilts, her jeweled boxes, and silk pillows in through our front door.

Billy groans. "Aunt Hortense is moving into the spare room."

"What!"

"Yep. To keep an eye on you."

"Me? What did I do?"

He rolls his eyes. "At least she's not making us move to her house. Remember when she used to do that?"

"What about Papa?"

"Apparently he's not going to be home for a while."

I look up at Noah's window. How will I get him his meals with Aunt Hortense watching?

Billy unhooks the traces and takes John Henry's collar off. I sponge down his sweat marks, pick up each of his big flat hooves to check for stones, and let him loose in his stall.

In our parlor, Papa's chair has been moved to make room for Aunt Hortense's French horn, her letter-writing pens, her magazines, her Bible, and a bell to call Maggy. Aunt Hortense stands waiting, dressed to go out, in a white dress with ruffles at the hem, the cuffs, and up and down her bodice. She has ribbons in her hair and a parasol in her hand.

"Why, Elizabeth"—she grinds the tip of the parasol into our rug—"where are your purchases?"

I look at her, try to smile. What is she talking about?

"The ones you bought at the Emporium."

"Oh, those. I didn't find anything," I say.

"Is that so?" She stares at me, waiting.

"There wasn't anything I liked." I can feel my nose growing longer with every word.

"We got a call from the police. You and William were trying to get into the Chinatown quarantine."

"No—"

"Elizabeth!" she barks.

"We weren't trying to get in," I whisper. "We were trying to get Jing out."

"They said you were using Mr. Sweeting's good name to curry favor."

Billy looks at me.

Aunt Hortense taps me with her parasol. "I won't be lied to."

"But Jing shouldn't be in there. It's wrong. If Papa were here, he'd get him out. We had to do something."

"In the first place, we have no idea if Jing is there or not. And in the second place, Mr. Sweeting has already agreed to help. Everything doesn't happen the instant you want it to, missy. But even more important than all of that . . . what if they do have the plague there?"

"We have to get Jing."

"You listen to me, young lady. Even without the quarantine, Chinatown is dangerous. You have no business going there, Jing or no Jing. Do you hear?"

Her stern eye falls on Billy. "And as for you, Master William." She taps her parasol on the rug, then the wooden floor, where it makes a more satisfying *clack.* "I expected more from you. Evidently neither of you can be trusted. While your father's gone, I'll be staying here so I can keep a closer watch on you."

"When's he coming back?" Billy asks.

"Next week," Aunt Hortense says.

"Next *week*?" I ask.

"He sent word by telegraph to the *Call* offices. There's a smallpox outbreak. A family with six children in San Rafael. He's got his hands full."

Papa has been immunized against smallpox, and so have Billy and I, but not everyone believes in immunization. If only they did, then he wouldn't have to be away so long. Why couldn't he just have an office here, the way Dr. Roumalade does?

I watch Aunt Hortense pin her hat. Her calendar is jam-packed with entertaining, committee meetings for charity events, doing the books for Uncle Karl and all the responsibilities of running a huge house with a staff of thirty-five. She won't be here all the time . . . will she?

"Mrs. Sweeting, where shall I stay?" red-haired, freckle-faced Nettie asks.

"In your own bed, Nettie. Maggy can handle me, can't you, Maggy?"

A smile flashes on Maggy's face.

"But, Mrs. Sweeting, ma'am, Maggy is not a ladies' maid. She hasn't been properly trained," Nettie grumbles.

"Well, then she'll learn, won't she?"

"I'm to teach her, then?"

"That would be lovely, Nettie."

On my windowsill is my collection of gifts from Jing. I run my hand over a smooth black stone carved with Mama's initials. There's the white feather from when I fell off Juliet and the rhyming dictionary with my mother's neat handwriting on the inside—Jing found that for me. On the end is the shell, with the word I misspelled from the spelling bee tucked inside. Jing said your mistakes teach you more than your victories.

Where is Jing now?

Maybe my note to Noah should warn him to be extra careful because Aunt Hortense is staying here now. But with the racket of all her stuff being moved in, not to mention her voice ringing through the house, he must know. Instead I write:

We've seen the quarantine. Monkey makes them wait. . . . Will investigate.

There's a block of cheese in the cold box. I cut a slab and drop it in my pocket. In Maggy's sewing basket, there were spools of thread, which I slipped into my top dresser drawer. Orange Tom is in my room, and I have his collar off. I fold up my message to Noah until it's the same width as Orange Tom's collar, then wrap green thread around the note and the collar until the paper is secure. Orange Tom scratches at the door of my room, trying to get out, his tail moving like a double-jointed finger. He smells of tuna fish.

I put his collar back and carry the sprawling cat to the servants' stairs, his back feet hanging down. I break off bits of cheese and toss them up the stairs while still holding the cat. The first piece falls short. It takes me five tries before I make it all the way up to the landing. With five pieces of cheese scattered along the servants' stairs, I'm confident the cat will go where I want him to. But when I release him, he leaps across the hall and down the main stairs.

It takes me the better part of an hour to catch him again. Now I close the second-floor hall door so he can't escape.

He runs straight up the servants' stairs to get away from me.

I'm listening for Noah's door to open, when Billy appears. He squints at me. "What are you doing with that cat?"

"Nothing."

"Why do you look so guilty?"

"I don't look guilty."

"You're hiding something. What is it?"

"Nothing." I try to go to my room, but he's blocking the door.

"You might as well tell me. You don't want me to find out on my own, do you?"

"Billy, there's nothing." I shove him out of my way and slam the door.

The Miracle of Dog Spit

In the morning, I run down and feed the horses and fill their water buckets. Then I consider pretending to be sick. But who wants to stay home with Aunt Hortense? Even Miss Barstow's is better than a day spent writing thank-you notes with Aunt Hortense.

How to get breakfast to Noah? Jing must have food in his room, but how much? Jing was expecting to be gone for two hours, but it's been two days. With Billy watching my every move and Aunt Hortense in command of the drawing room, I couldn't get Noah supper last night.

Luckily, Billy leaves for school before I do. I only have Aunt Hortense to worry about now. Down in the kitchen, the Sweetings' chef, Yang Sun, has brought over croissants and brioche, jams and jellies, honey-butter, clotted cream, and long baguettes baked with ham and cheese—more food than we could ever eat. I grab a pitcher of water and wrap two croissants and a brioche in a tea towel, but when I go outside, the cord is not down.

In the dining room, Aunt Hortense is drinking her tea and reading the morning paper, with Maggy standing beside her. "Ready?" Aunt Hortense asks.

"No," I say, and rush upstairs to my room, where I leave my bundle of pastries and compose my message. After a few tries, I come up with: *There's a meal. On the stair. If you dare.* Then I grab blue thread from the drawer and begin searching for the orange cat. I find him in the stable loft, curled up in a bed of straw, next to a dead mouse. He eyes me warily as I unbuckle his collar, which I now see has white thread around it.

Noah sent a message back!

His message is written in black ink on bumpy rice paper. He has made a little drawing of a monkey.

The monkey has a secret.

What does that mean? And what if Aunt Hortense intercepts this note? How will I explain it?

Then I smile. Aunt Hortense is allergic, of course! She won't touch Orange Tom. It's only Billy I have to worry about.

I attach the new message with blue thread. The cat lets his muscles go limp. I carry him down the loft ladder, his legs bumping against mine as I make my way down the rungs. I lug the big fat cat all the way to the house.

I peek through the window. The kitchen is empty. Yang Sun does his cooking in the Sweeting kitchen. Ours is too small for him.

Just as I get Orange Tom in the kitchen, Aunt Hortense sashays across the cold storage room with Nettie and Maggy right behind her. Maggy is carrying a linen pouch full of Aunt Hortense's hair. Each time Maggy brushes her hair, the hairs from the brush must be saved in the bag. She's keeping it to make a hairpiece, should the need arise.

"Maggy," Nettie says. "I'll take that now."

Maggy hands her the bag, and Nettie scoots out the kitchen door.

Aunt Hortense looks up. "Elizabeth, don't you dare bring that dreadful creature in here. I'll be sneezing all day."

"Oh, I forgot," I say as she streaks into the dining room away from the cat, Maggy flying after her. Now Maggy has a teacup and saucer and a box of menus. Aunt Hortense writes two menus every day, one for the family and one for the servants. She even plans out tea and snacks.

If Aunt Hortense is doing menus, she'll stay put for a while. I go back out and around the house to the front door, then dash up the stairs with the cat. But just as I do, Nettie comes back.

"Didn't you hear Mrs. Sweeting? No cats."

I pretend to clean the wax out of my ears. "Oh, um," I say, and head back out.

"Bad enough I got to watch that Maggy," she grumbles. "She's been hearing things. She ain't right in the mind, that one."

Orange Tom tries to wiggle out of my arms, but I hold him tight. "What things?"

"From Jing's room when he ain't there."

Oh, great.

Nettie squints at me. "You know something about that?"

"It's just the cat. He likes to go up there."

"Cat should be made into a handbag, if you ask me," Nettie mutters.

I wait until Nettie is gone, then make another run up the stairs with Orange Tom. In my room, I get Noah's tea-towel-wrapped pastries. I place the bundle on the servants' stairs, then toss the cheese up and close the second-floor hall door, so Tom will be forced up to the third floor. If Aunt Hortense or Nettie finds the brioche and croissants, I'll say I planned to take them to school to share with the other girls and I forgot them when I was sitting on the stairs button-hooking my boots.

The water pitchers! If they all disappear, it will be suspicious. I have to remember to bring them back down. It's exhausting thinking of lies Aunt Hortense will believe. But she can't find out about Noah. She'll have him arrested, whether he's Jing's son or not.

Today at Miss Barstow's, the girls are in the dining room. The topic seems to be the move to Presidio Heights. Miss Barstow has found a fancier place for the school. And everybody wonders if that means we'll be wearing uniforms, which of course leads to the topic of bustles. How big should they be? Which ones ride up when you sit down and which don't?

I sit by myself as usual. My book and me. For a second, I think about what Noah said. Is there one girl I like better than the rest? Nope.

The girls giggle, the metronome pings, a dog barks, and the same three chords are pounded on the piano. I try to concentrate on the story, but all I can think about is Noah.

The barking continues. Miss Barstow would never allow a dog in the house. I walk out of the dining room and up the thickly carpeted stairs toward the sound. If you're caught hurrying, you must recite the class motto, "All things come to him who waits," and freeze while everyone passes you by. At the very least shouldn't it be: "All things come to he who waits"?

In the geography room, old maps cover the walls, wood floors clack under my boots, and the dunce cap waits for its next victim. Gemma is plunked down on the floor, crutches splayed out beside her.

"Gemma? Did you fall?"

Gemma barks.

"Wait. You're the dog?"

Gemma licks her hand, and then rotates her arm around her ear, like a canine itching with its back leg. "Shhh, Gemma! If Miss Barstow hears you, she'll pitch a fit."

"A dog bit me this morning. I have rabies." Gemma tips back her head and howls.

"Rabies? You can't get rabies that quickly."

"How would you know?"

"My father's a doctor."

"Really?" Her arm drops down.

All I know about Gemma is that she often asks me what I'm reading and the other girls like her a lot.

I help her up and hand her her crutches. She fits them under her armpits just as Miss Barstow rings the bell.

Gemma smiles. I look around to see who has come up behind me.

No one. She's smiling at me. I can't help grinning back.

"Time for dance class," I say.

"You like to dance?"

I hate to dance. It's worse than swallowing cod liver oil. Last week, when Gemma wasn't here, Miss Annabelle called me Horse Feet, and the girls all laughed. Why am I nodding?

"Miss Barstow says I'm not allowed to."

"You're on crutches," I point out.

"So?"

I want to talk to her as long as I can, before the other girls arrive and I become invisible. "Did you really get bitten by a rabid dog?"

"It may have been more of a hard lick."

"A hard lick?" I try not to laugh.

She leans in. "Can you get rabies from dog spit?"

Is this a joke? Every time I laugh at something a girl at Miss Barstow's says, I get weird looks. "I wouldn't think so . . . unless the dog licks an open wound."

She looks down at her wrist. Her shoulders droop.

"You *want* rabies, Gemma?"

"No." She plants her crutches and swings her body to meet them. I follow her to the dance studio and stand with her. When the others come, I'll lose this spot. But now only the little girls are here.

"Ring around the rosie, pocket full of posies. Ashes, ashes, they all fall down." They collapse in a heap.

"Why do they fall on the floor like that?" I ask.

"They're dead."

"From what?"

"The plague."

"Nice," I say.

Gemma laughs.

I stare at her.

She frowns. "What's the matter?"

"You laughed."

"So?"

I tip my head at the girls streaming through the door. "They never laugh."

Her eyes look deep inside me. "They're all right," she whispers. "You should give them a chance."

I should give *them* a chance?

"They're not sure what to say to you, that's all," Gemma whispers as Miss Barstow swoops into the room to begin her lesson.

"San Francisco is the Paris of the Pacific, and every young woman must know the language, the dances, and the culture. French restaurants have taken over the city. French clothes are all the rage, and any one of us might marry a Frenchman with a title—a duke or a baron." Miss

Barstow sails across the floor, her back as straight as a scalpel, her steel-gray hair tightly pinned. The mole on her lip is the only part of her that seems unplanned.

"Listen, please, ladies," she says, but my eyes are on Gemma. Even with the other girls here, Gemma hasn't backed away from me.

"When a gentleman approaches you at the cotillion, what might you say to spark a conversation?" Miss Barstow asks.

The weather, music, hunting, his schooling. The usual answers.

"I'd ask, were you a bed wetter?" I whisper. But as soon as I do, I regret it. My tongue is like an enemy in my mouth.

Gemma peeks at me, eyes sparkling.

I keep going. "No shame in it," I whisper. "George Washington was a bed wetter."

Gemma flaps her hand over her mouth to keep from laughing, just as the elocution teacher pokes her head in the door and motions to Miss Barstow.

"He could have been," I tell her when Miss Barstow ducks out of the room. "We don't know. What biographer is going to write about that? Or you could ask your gentleman friend what runs in his family—madness? Apoplexy?"

"What about that crazy aunt locked in the attic?" Gemma asks. "Every family has one."

Hattie with the pouty lips is watching. She can't believe Gemma is sharing secrets with me.

Miss Barstow is back. "Dr. Roumalade is here for our annual health examinations. Gemma, you're first. Please go to my office."

Hattie leaps across the room to hold the door open. Two other girls walk with Gemma.

Miss Annabelle is running the class now. We're learning a new dance. I write down the instructions in my notebook to appear to be paying attention—a technique I use often.

When Gemma comes back, I've faded into the wall. She heads straight for me. "Your turn," she says.

Why would I need an examination? My father's a doctor. Still, I'm stupidly happy Gemma chose me.

Dr. Roumalade has powdery hands, a round head, cheeks as red as raw steak, and a slender mustache. He smiles pleasantly. "Jules Kennedy's daughter, if I'm not mistaken. And how is your father?"

"Fine, sir."

He slips his stethoscope around his neck. "I understand you've been accompanying him on his calls." The flat metal disk presses against my chest as he listens to my heart through the connecting tube.

"Yes, sir." How does he know this?

"He doesn't have an assistant?"

"No, sir."

"I couldn't handle my practice without one."

I bristle.

He's inspecting my ears now. I can feel his finger and hear a *whoosh* sound inside my ear. He looks into my eyes and peers down my throat. "Interested in nursing, are you?"

"No, sir. I'm going to be a scientist."

He snorts. "You mean you'll marry a scientist. Any persistent coughing, diarrhea, fever, headaches?"

"No, sir."

He washes his hands in the bowl Miss Barstow has provided. His examination isn't as thorough as Papa's. "You, my dear, are as healthy as a horse. I will let your aunt and uncle know."

"The Sweetings? Why?"

"Going hither and yon with all manner of clientele."

"What does that have to do with Aunt Hortense and Uncle Karl?"

"With you accompanying your father the way you have, he puts you at risk."

"No, he doesn't!"

"Certainly you understand contagion, my dear."

My fingers curl into a fist. "My father does not put me at risk."

"You think you know everything, do you?" Dr. Roumalade presses the tips of his fingers together. "But you don't. The dangers are real."

"Papa takes good care of me."

Dr. Roumalade presses his lips together. "Well . . . thank you for calming Gemma Trotter down. She has quite the imagination."

"She's doing fine."

"Yes. Now, you say hello to your father for me. He's a good doctor. It's a shame he doesn't have a busier practice."

My cheeks burn. "My father is doing very well."

"I always try to refer patients to him."

Right. If a patient isn't able to pay. A lot of help that is.

I count backward from ten to keep from saying what I shouldn't.

"All right, then, Lizzie. We're done here."

Miss Barstow must be listening at the door, because she comes right in. "Go tell Kathryn she's next. Quickly, please."

I'm just turning the corner when I hear Dr. Roumalade tell Miss Barstow:

"You've got your work cut out for you with that one, Sarah."

"It's the age."

"I suppose."

When I get back to class, Gemma is in a huddle with Hattie and the other girls. Do I dare stand with her?

It's better to choose to be alone than to try to be friends with someone who doesn't want to be your friend. I go to my usual spot, six feet from everyone else, though a tiny part of me knows that I'm taking the chicken's way out.

"Lizzie!" Gemma waves me over. "Why are you over there? C'mon with us," she says.

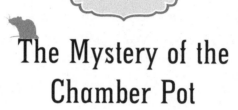

The Mystery of the Chamber Pot

When I get home, I run to the front yard, where I have a clear view of Noah's window. The blind is down, the window a uniform gray. No gold cord hangs over the top.

If only I could wish that stupid cord down.

"Peanut."

I jump, Uncle Karl is leaning against a tree, cigar smoke swirling around him. Is he watching me?

"What's so interesting up there?"

"Nothing."

"Nothing, huh?" He leans his chin on his hand.

"What are you doing out here?" I try to turn the tables.

"Waiting for Billy," he says. "And you?"

"Looking for the cat."

"The cat?" Uncle Karl's eyes cut through me.

My hands are shaking as I search for Orange Tom. Uncle Karl is never in our yard. Does he know something?

On the way back from the barn, I spot a dead rat under the hedge, so Orange Tom must be around. I go up to my room. I don't want to run into Uncle Karl again.

Upstairs, I begin thinking about Gemma Trotter. Why was she nice to me today? Is she the person Noah said I should look for, the one I like better than the rest? I can't wait to tell Noah what happened. I won't say anything about Uncle Karl, though. I don't want to scare him. I focus on finding words that rhyme with "Gemma."

Today a girl named Gemma
Had quite a big dilemma.
She barked like a dog with babies,
On account of she thought she had rabies.
At nine o'clock they talked to the doc.
"It's all in her head" is what he said.

I run down to see if the cord is visible. Still no.

In the pantry, I collect as much food as possible, in case I can't get back up there for a while. I fill a basket with mason jars of pears, peaches, applesauce, and olives, a hunk of cheese, a roll of salami, and half a loaf of French bread.

And water. I fill a pitcher, but it won't fit in the basket. I make two trips to my room to get it all up there. Just as I'm carrying the pitcher filled to the brim, Aunt Hortense appears. In her hand is a wad of dollar bills.

"Maggy, dear!" she calls down the stairs. "Can you iron

these for me? I can't stand to carry those filthy things all bunched up like that. Elizabeth? What are you doing? Maggy filled that this morning."

"I wanted more . . . in case of fire," I add lamely.

"Fire? Goodness gracious, child, what makes you worry about that?"

"We talked about it at Miss Barstow's."

She nods. "Speaking of worrying, I talked to Mr. Sweeting. He's working on finding Jing."

"Thank you," I say.

She shimmies her hands into her gloves.

"You're going out?"

"Try not to sound so happy. Mrs. Luther Cumberbatch is taking me out driving in her very own motorcar. A woman with a driver's license—can you imagine? Yang Sun will bring your supper over."

"Yes, ma'am."

"And, Lizzie . . . no trouble while I'm gone."

"Yes, ma'am."

She takes my chin in her gloved hand. "Don't just move your lips."

I look her straight in the eye. "No trouble," I say.

I carry the pitcher into my room and close the door, then watch out the window. I hear the motorcar before I see it. It roars into the driveway, then spits and gasps to a stop. Aunt Hortense climbs in, decked out in a pale green driving dress edged in velvet, her dark hair glistening under her green wide-brimmed hat tightly secured with a white veil. Mrs. Cumberbatch is wearing a plaid driving coat and matching hat. Aunt Hortense waves to her butler, who cranks the motor again. The car sputters forward, lurching through the gate.

When they're gone, I run outside and check for the cord. It's finally down! Noah must have seen her leave, too.

Maggy is on the side porch in a cloud of dust, beating a rug and grunting. The parrot is on her shoulder. "Dirty work. Dirty work," Mr. P. chirps. Billy has gone off with Uncle Karl.

Nobody notices me as I make my stealthy trips, bringing supplies to Noah.

When we get everything inside and the door closed, we smile at each other. "How long do you think we have?" he asks.

"Hard to say."

I sit on the chair. He sits on the bed.

I fill him in on what happened at Chinatown. "We tried to get Jing out."

"You and Billy?"

I nod. "I talked to a policeman. He was no help. But Uncle Karl is working on it. Aunt Hortense said."

Noah sighs, his brow furrowed. "I know he's there."

"Does he do magic shows for people in Chinatown?" I ask.

He frowns at me. "No."

Jing does magic shows for Billy and me. Why wouldn't he do them for the people in Chinatown?

"Leaders don't do magic tricks," Noah explains.

I try to imagine Jing as a leader of people in Chinatown. This is not the Jing I know.

"I thought you said he was a translator."

He nods. "It's a powerful position. Hardly anyone understands the language and customs of both sides. Chinese don't understand Americans. Americans don't understand Chinese. Nobody trusts anyone. It's a big mess."

"What did you mean, 'The monkey has a secret'?"

"Baba must have told you his stories."

"About animals?"

He nods. "Whenever there's a monkey, he's a trickster with secrets up his sleeve. You never know if his secrets will help the good guys or the bad ones."

"Are there any real monkeys in Chinatown?"

He shakes his head. "There's a year of the monkey, but that was a while ago. This year is the year of the rat."

"The year of the rat. Who picks these animals?"

He shrugs. "Somebody made a calendar a thousand years ago."

"Hey," I say. "I wrote a poem. Want to see?"

I hand him Gemma's poem. He reads it carefully. "She thought she had rabies? That's crazy."

"Yes."

"But you like her better than the others?"

I suck my lip, considering.

"You do." He nods, then leans forward. "Have you written a poem about me?"

"Not yet." He wants me to write him a poem! What will I say? I get up and begin poking around his room. "What do you do in here all day?"

"Read, mostly. Watch out the window. Sew the buttonhole strips. When Orange Tom comes up, we play a game with a ball of thread."

"You play with the cat?"

"Sure. Don't you?"

"No. I don't like the cat. Hey," I whisper. "How do you . . . you know? We're not allowed to use the second-floor toilet. It's only for guests and Aunt Hortense."

His face turns just slightly red. "I know that."

"Do you sneak out at night to empty your chamber pot?"

"No."

"Pour it out the window?" I stand up and slide across to the window to peek under the blind. What will the pee fall on?

"Disgusting."

"Store it up?" I turn back around to sniff the air.

"Are you always this nosey?"

I grin at him. "Pretty much."

He sighs. "It's none of your business."

"Well, then I'll have to find out, won't I?"

"How are you going to do that? Follow me everywhere?"

I walk around the room inspecting tea cups, bowls, a vase.

He grins. "You don't think I go in there, do you?"

"You'll have to go eventually," I say.

"Nope. I'm special."

"You know I'm going to find out."

He crosses his arms and juts out his chin. "You are not."

We both burst out laughing.

"For a girl, you sure are pushy."

"But you like me. We're friends now." I grin at him.

He nods, his brown eyes serious. "You know we're not

allowed to be friends. Not out there." He points to the window.

"We decide if we're going to be friends. Not them," I insist, though inside I'm not so sure. The world seems more complicated than it ever has before.

Backward Day

No lights are on at the Sweeting house. Not even the rooster is out of bed yet. I creep down to the kitchen to put together a plate of fried potatoes from last night, two oranges, what's left of the bread, and a jar of water. With a full basket, I sneak halfway up the servants' stairs, far enough down that Maggy or Noah will not see me. Everybody in the world has to pee first thing in the morning. Noah will steal down to the second-floor bathroom, and I'll catch him. If Maggy comes down or Aunt Hortense comes up, I'll tell them . . . its backward day and I'm bringing Maggy her breakfast instead of the other way around.

I wait so long that I doze off on the stairs, waking with a start when I hear Juliet whinny. Up above I hear the *click-flap, click-flap* of Maggy's loose-soled boots. A door closes, then opens. I sneak up the last few stairs to see what's happening.

Out the hall window, the sun is rising, a bright orange ball between fluffy gray clouds. Inside, it's just the same as it always is, except a white chamber pot is outside Maggy's door. Is it Noah's? Is Maggy emptying it? But Maggy doesn't know about Noah.

Maggy must put hers outside her door while she gets dressed, and then I'm betting Noah pours his into hers.

I try to imagine what it's like to have to be so careful that you can't smack your lips, talk in your sleep, or hop out of bed. No coughing, laughing, or stepping on a creaky board. You can't breathe too loudly, open the window, or pee too much.

I decide not to leave the food now. I should wait until Maggy comes down first. I'm carrying the basket down the stairs when I trip on the last step and fall flat on my face.

Before I can get up, Billy appears, his hair uncombed, his chin unshaved.

He surveys the spilled potatoes, watches as I chase after the orange that rolls across the floor. "What are you doing?"

"It's backward day. I was bringing Maggy breakfast."

"Didn't she want it?"

"Oh. Um. She ate some of it already," I say, cleaning up the mess, throwing it all haphazardly back in the basket.

Billy's left shoulder is wrapped in a towel, held tight with his right hand.

"What happened?" I ask.

He unwraps the towel. His shoulder is badly bruised, and there's crusty brown blood making it hard to see the wound.

I reach out, but he steps back. "How'd you do it?"

"Just woke up this way." He winks with his good eye.

I survey his clothes. He hasn't been to bed yet.

"Let's get it cleaned up."

Billy follows me into my room and sits on my bed. I set the basket down on my dresser doily, pour water from the pitcher onto a towel, and gently pat the dried blood away. After the cleaning, it doesn't look so bad. Just one snaggly wound line and some bruising and swelling.

"Needs stitches," I observe. I've never done sutures by myself. I bet I could, though.

"I'll do it," Billy says.

"On yourself?"

"Sure. Could you get the suture kit?"

I run down to get the kit, along with ice, a clean rag, towels, and a bandage roll. Jing stacks the clean rolls in a tin box. I never realized just how much Jing does for us, until now. Does he know how much we miss him?

"Thanks," Billy says when I bring the supplies back to my room. He lays a towel on the bed. I watch him clean the wound area with a rag. He ices the skin around the cut and then threads the suture needle. He takes a deep breath, his needle hand wavering, then sticks it into the skin and pulls through.

I can't watch this anymore. I sit down next to him on my bed and take the needle from him. "Can you cough?"

He nods. He's seen Papa do this trick as many times as I have. A cough distracts a patient from the pain.

"On the count of three. One, two, three." He coughs, and I stick the needle in.

I pull the thread through and tie it off. "How was that?"

"Not bad."

He breathes in, I count, he coughs, and I stick the needle in. I'm glad he needs only five stitches. When I'm done, he takes the thread from me, cuts it, splits it in half, and ties it off—all with one hand.

He could be a doctor if he wanted to.

"Do you want me to bandage it?" I ask.

He nods, and I begin to wind Jing's bandage around the stitches.

"Not so tight," he whispers.

I loosen the wrap.

When I'm done, he shoots me one of his glittering Billy smiles, and I hope, hope, hope the old Billy is back.

Gently, I inspect his black eye. It's healing nicely. "Billy? Why are you so angry?"

"Why are you sneaking around the third floor?"

I swallow hard. "I'm not." I try to keep my expression neutral.

"Okay, then," he whispers. "I'm not angry, and you're not hiding something on the third floor."

"I'm not hiding anything."

"Uncle Karl thinks you are."

My stomach drops. "He does?"

Billy nods. "There's a cat with kittens up there, right?" He stands up, ready to leave.

"Right."

Billy laughs. "Orange Tom has been busy."

I nod too enthusiastically.

"Everybody has secrets . . . even Orange Tom."

"Papa doesn't believe in secrets," I say.

"Papa is a good man."

"Why are you so mad at him all the time, then?"

Billy shrugs. "He expects too much. I'm not like him."

"I'm not like him, either."

"You're more like him than I am. I'm like Mama. She liked to have fun. With Papa you have to do the right thing every minute of every day. He never lets up."

After Billy leaves, I wait until Maggy comes down. Then I put the food out. Noah will get it before Maggy goes back up to her room. But even if he doesn't, I've already explained that this is backward day. I'll say I left the food for her. It's worth the risk. Noah has to eat.

The Sweetings' stable boy, Ho, drives me to school, but drops me off in the wrong place and I have to go back around. Jing always knows the right way to do everything. Strange how you assume everybody does, and then you realize, no, it's just Jing.

By the time I get there, Gemma is sitting with Hattie like always. If I go back to my old table, everything will be the way it always has been. I'll never have to worry that I've said the wrong thing or that Gemma likes Hattie better than me. My feet walk me back to my old spot. I am a big chicken.

"Lizzie!" Gemma hops over, not bothering with her crutches, and plunks down in the chair beside me. Hattie does an arabesque and then slides into the seat on my other side.

"We're going to Ocean Beach after school. Can you come?" Gemma asks.

I open my mouth to say no. I have other things to do.

"Pretty please." She puts her hands together like she's praying. The other girls watch me, not sure why Gemma's acting this way.

"You'll ride with me," Gemma announces, as if I've agreed. "We'll pick you up at three."

How will I spend the whole afternoon with them? What will we talk about? I can't do this, but my head is nodding yes and my mouth is saying "Thank you."

When I get home, I head for the Sweeting house to find Uncle Karl. It's been three days. He must have found out something about Jing by now. I can't tell Noah there's no news again.

Uncle Karl is out, but Aunt Hortense is here working her arithmometer.

She looks up from the brown box. "You need something?"

"Has Uncle Karl found Jing?"

"Not that I know of. But, honey, don't you think Jing would have gotten word to us if he were stuck in the quarantine?"

"How could he? They won't let anyone out."

"Jing is a resourceful man. He'd have found a way. I'm just wondering if he got another job."

"Another job? Not Jing!"

"It happens," Aunt Hortense says.

"You don't want him to come back. You think he's infectious."

"Of course I want Jing back."

I watch her as she flips the page in the ledger.

"Is it okay if I go to Ocean Beach this afternoon? The girls from Miss Barstow's are all going. Gemma Trotter's papa is driving us in their horseless carriage."

Aunt Hortense looks up in surprise. A smiles sneaks across her lips. "That would be fine. Have fun, Elizabeth."

Astral Dog

Mr. Trotter beams as I climb into his motorcar. He wipes down the dust that accumulated on his drive to my house. Motorcars are stinky, slow, and unreliable. Horses will get you where you want to go, safely and on time. They won't run you into a brick wall the way a brainless hunk of metal will.

I sit in the back between Gemma and her twin brother, Gus. Gus has the same red-blond hair as Gemma, but he's tall and thin, with a prominent Adam's apple. I can't help grinning. Gemma chose me to drive with! Hattie isn't even here. Gemma chatters the whole way there, but I can hardly hear over the racket of the motorcar.

At the Cliff House, the big restaurant above the beach, Mr. Trotter jumps out to check the tires, and we pile out.

"Gus?" Mr. Trotter stands up, one eye still on the tire. "I thought you were coming with me?"

Gus's eyes are glued to his bootlaces. He blushes a splotchy red.

Mr. Trotter looks from Gus to me, then to Gus again. "Look after the girls, would you, Son? Meet me at the front entrance at half past four."

Gemma is so excited, she races on her crutches. "Wait until you see this! Just wait!" When she gets to the stairs, she places her crutches cautiously on each step, then hops down.

Gus follows, his hands shoved deep into his pockets.

Down on the boardwalk, we walk by match peddlers, bootblacks, singing newsboys, and the rows of cages of Johnnie-the-Birdman. Johnnie-the-Birdman has singing birds and a canary that pulls a tiny cannon string, which makes a popgun sound. Another bird pretends to fall over dead. Gus and I laugh, but Gemma pulls us along. She has something else in mind.

The wind whips my hat, my boots sink into the sand, the Cliff House band *oom-pah-pah*s behind us as a purse-size dog chases a rat under the boardwalk. Gemma stays on the wooden walkway, as far from the rat as possible. Rat or no rat, she can't manage sand with her crutches.

Up ahead, a small crowd forms around a tall man with dark hair and a long nose, who is standing on a makeshift stage. Hattie and a few of the other girls from Miss Barstow's stand near the front.

ASTRAL DOG, the sign says, between pictures of celestial planets and shooting stars.

"He's here!" Gemma hops on her one good foot.

The man on the stage is wearing a purple velvet suit, a blue plaid vest, and shiny pointy-toed blue shoes. An ill-fitted bowler hat is perched on his head. "Come see the world's only matchmaking canine," he calls.

Astral Dog is a small brown-and-white terrier dressed in a blue cape and a blue turban with cutouts for his small furry folded-over ears.

"If your true love is among us, Astral Dog will find him." The little dog dances on his hind legs. "He, and only he, will recognize your future betrothed.

"But sometimes, sadly, your true love is not here." Astral Dog's head sinks low, his tail goes down between his legs, his dog shoulders slump.

"If you are not lonely—if you have never been lonely—walk on by, sir. Walk on by." Astral Dog jumps off the stage to work the crowd, standing on his hind legs, his turban held in place with a ribbon strap. The velvet man follows behind, collecting nickels.

Gemma's eyes are on a boy with a thick blond thatch of hair, blue eyes, and big white teeth.

Hattie hurries over to where we stand on the boardwalk. "Spencer," Hattie whispers to me as the boy drops his nickel into the velvet man's hat.

Gemma grabs my arm. "We have to get tickets," she whispers.

"I already have," Hattie says, and does a pirouette.

"You go ahead," I tell Gemma. They can get tickets. I'll just watch.

"But more often than not, lonely people are brought together and two hearts become one." Astral Dog and the velvet man return to the stage. He brings his arms together, forming a heart with his hands, and I slink back into the crowd away from Hattie and Gemma.

The dog sits up, one ear cocked to the sky. "If you wish to meet your soul's match, your heart's companion, it costs but a nickel. Think of it. . . . A nickel, little lady, can alter the course of your entire life."

Astral Dog jumps down and begins to dance in front of Gemma Trotter.

Gemma's cheeks flush. She unties a corner of her hankie and takes out two nickels. "For us." She looks around, then points me out to the velvet man.

"Gemma!" I cry.

Too late. The nickels are in the hat and the man has moved on. "The list of happy couples, matches divined by Astral Dog." He unfurls a long scroll of names in wildly intricate handwriting.

Gemma motions for me to come back. I'm standing next to her now. "Don't you want to dance?" she whispers.

I think I'm going to be sick.

"How are *you* going to dance?" I whisper. I'm worried about Gemma, but I'm more worried about me. Everyone will see. Hattie will make fun of me. Gemma won't want to be friends after that.

"I'll be fine," Gemma says.

More people crowd forward. Even the balloon man offers up a nickel, balloons dipping and bobbing as he digs it out. The velvet man's hat clinks with coins. "Yes, the time has come, ladies and gentleman. The celestial bodies are in alignment."

With a dramatic flourish, the velvet man produces a tiny dog-size desk and a mini crystal ball from a large velvet bag. He sets the ball on the desk and places the dog's red throne front center of the stage.

Astral Dog hops onto his throne to peer at the crystal ball, and the audience cheers, thrilled the show is beginning.

Having seen the match in the crystal ball, Astral Dog winds his way among us, sniffing our boots. He stops in front of a lady with a hat the size of a small house, but when she offers the dog her ticket, he moves on without taking it and heads straight for Gemma.

"What is your name, please?" the velvet man asks.

"But I don't want to be first!"

"The acts of providence are beyond our control."

"Gemma Trotter," she whispers.

"Gem-ma! Gem-ma!" Hattie and the other girls clap and chant. The whole crowd is calling.

Gemma screws up her face like she's swallowing bad medicine. She takes a big brave breath, opens her eyes, and offers her ticket to Astral Dog. The little dog takes it delicately between his teeth, and then follows the velvet man back to the desk, watching the man as he describes the difficult process of divining celestial matches. Then the man and the dog walk up and down the line of boys with tickets in their hands.

When Astral Dog reaches Spencer, the dog sits, cocks his head, and waits for Spencer to take the ticket.

Aha! Gemma's secret looks in the direction of Spencer have not gone unnoticed.

The velvet man plays his harmonica, but Spencer doesn't take Gemma's hand.

"He don't know what to do," someone shouts.

"Dance around her," the balloon man suggests.

"Take her hand."

"Go on, now. Just dance!" The calls come from all around.

But Spencer stands, as stupid as a hitching post.

The crowd begins to murmur. Nobody likes this. Finally the velvet man signals the dog, who does a dance around Gemma. When the harmonica stops, Spencer can't get off the stage fast enough.

Gemma's eyes fill up. She bites her lip and stares at her boots.

I leap onto the stage to give Gemma her crutches, but just as I do, Astral Dog turns to me, his tail wagging so hard, it drags his bottom with it.

"Astral Dog has found his next happy couple." The velvet man is eager to move on. No one will pay for more tickets after a match like Gemma and Spencer's.

"Lizzie." Gemma blinks back her tears and grabs my hand. "That's you."

My face flushes. I'm too tall for the boys. My feet are larger than theirs are.

"But, Gemma," I whisper. "I can't dance."

Gus glances at me. Gemma frowns. "Don't be silly." She snatches my ticket and offers it to Astral Dog—who chomps it happily, then works his way through the paying customers and stops in front of Gus. Gus steals a look in my direction and then motions to the velvet man.

The two confer in whispers, and then the velvet man's head pops up. "Sadly," he says, "the dance cannot occur due to unforeseen circumstances." The crowd begins to boo, but the velvet man cries, "And yet the match remains strong." Gus bows to me, saluting with his hat. I try to curtsy as Gemma claps.

Gus's manner is polite and kind, and the crowd's boos turn to whistles and claps. Astral Dog does his dance, and the velvet man moves on to the next match.

Gemma points her crutch at her brother. "What was that about?"

Gus's eyes find mine, then dart away. "I didn't feel like dancing, and neither did she," he mutters, pink all the way down his long neck.

We walk back to the Cliff House, where men in straw boater hats are drinking and laughing. While we're waiting for Mr. Trotter, a lady dressed in pink bursts out the door of the restaurant, followed by a small sour man. Her face is flushed. She fans herself wildly. "Air. A little fresh air and I'll be fine." She tries to smile. Then suddenly she rushes over to a potted palm and throws up.

Stomach flu? Food poisoning? An allergic reaction? If only Papa were here. He'd know what to do. I'm trying to think how to help, when Mr. Trotter comes out. He takes in the scene with his quick eyes. "Let's get out of here," he barks.

CHAPTER 15

Doh Je

When I get home, Aunt Hortense is in our drawing room making lists of who to call for the children's bazaar. "How was Ocean Beach?"

"Fine."

"That's all you're going to say?"

"I had a nice time with Gemma. Do you know where Uncle Karl is?"

"In his study, but approach him at your own risk. He's not in the best of moods."

"Shall I wait until tomorrow?"

"You could, but he's got his big newspaper luncheon tomorrow. Day after tomorrow is my recommendation."

"That's too late."

She shrugs. "Don't say I didn't warn you."

I walk over to the big house and upstairs to Uncle Karl's large high-ceilinged office. On one wall he has dowels with newspapers hanging on them. The *Chronicle,* the *Call,* the *Examiner,* and *Chung Sai Yat Po,* the Chinese newspaper. On another wall, he has awards and photos of him with famous people such as Leland Stanford, Governor Gage, and President McKinley. Uncle Karl knows everyone. On the back wall are photos of S&S Sugar and big blocks of movable type with his name, Aunt Hortense's name, my name, and Billy's name.

"Peanut"—he looks up from the paper—"are you coming to visit me, or do you need something?"

If I say I'm here to visit him, I'm a liar. If I say I want something, I'm a louse.

Uncle Karl seems to know my answer before I open my mouth. "Because, you know what, I get tired of being a screwdriver."

"I can see why, sir," I offer.

"Can you?" He straightens the ink blotter on his desk.

I nod.

"And you'll remember that in the future, but today you need something. You want to know if I found out anything about Jing. . . . Am I right?"

I stare down at his bearskin rug.

"He's vanished, so far as I can tell," Uncle Karl says.

"He's not in Chinatown?" My eyelid begins to twitch.

"I've let Mrs. Sweeting know she is to begin interviewing cooks for you."

"What?"

"Yang Sun can't continue to cook for both households."

"But Jing is in the quarantine."

"How exactly do you know this?"

I'd love to tell him how. But of course I don't. "I just think he is, that's all. Anyway, the quarantine is supposed to be over soon, so he'll come home." I make this up.

"It is, is it?" He smiles. A nice smile? Or a mean one? "You're an authority on the subject?"

"They were waiting on the monkey," I explain.

He stubs his cigar in the ashtray. "You don't know what you're talking about, Lizzie. And where did you hear about that anyway?"

"I don't know."

He snorts. "You don't know? Wise to keep your mouth shut, if you know nothing about a subject."

"Tell me about the monkey."

"There's nothing to tell."

I cock my head and look at him. "Why are you so grumpy about it, then?"

"Don't stick your nose where it doesn't belong, Lizzie," he booms.

"Yes, sir."

He hangs up one newspaper and takes down another. His back is to me.

Boy, was Aunt Hortense ever right. No talking to Uncle Karl when he's in a mood. I head downstairs, grinding my teeth.

But why did me asking about the monkey make him so angry? And besides that, they can't hire a new cook.

A new cook would live in Jing's room. Then what would Noah do?

In my room, I look at Jing's presents again. What if Jing is really gone? I'll never get another gift from him, my birthday cakes will have nothing inside, and I will never have another banana pancake.

I find my fountain pen and paper. Noah will help me figure this out.

Egad, our monkey made him mad.
What does Karl know?
Is he friend or foe?

I decide not to mention what Karl said about interviewing for a new cook. I don't want Noah to think all girls are liars, but he might panic if I tell him. I need to talk to Aunt Hortense. She'll be doing the interviewing. She's the one I have to get on my side.

First, find the cat. I head out to the barn and climb up into the loft, where he's curled up in the corner, his usual spot. The thread color on his collar is yellow. A message from Noah!

I unwrap the rice paper and slip it out. It has Chinese characters this time. And the words *"Doh je."*

Doh je? What does that mean? I pocket his note and attach mine with blue thread. Then I haul the cat down the ladder. He squirms out of my arms, leaps into the haystack, shoots across the barn, and jumps onto the divider between the stalls, which he walks like an acrobat. I lunge for him; the tips of my fingers graze his fur. He streaks across to the chicken coop. I chase after him; he runs, then stops and watches me. His eyes track my every move.

I stalk him until I get close enough to scoop him up. He allows himself to be caught only when he's good and ready. I run into the kitchen for cheese, then carry him into Papa's library, where I think there is a Chinese-English dictionary. With the cheese, the cat, and the phrasebook, I head back to my room.

The cat stands by the door while I page through the dictionary. *"Doh je"* means "thank you." I look for a few other words while I'm at it.

Uncle Karl said he didn't like being a screwdriver. I wouldn't like that, either. But when you help a friend, it just feels good.

CHAPTER 16

Monkey in the Garden

At breakfast, I corner Aunt Hortense. "Are you really going to hire a cook to replace Jing?"

"Oh, Elizabeth . . ."

"Mama hired Jing. He's a part of our family. She wouldn't like it."

Aunt Hortense's hand freezes on her teacup. "When Mr. Sweeting asks me to do something, I do it. Your mama of all people would understand that. One day, you'll get married, and this will all make sense to you."

"I'm never getting married."

Aunt Hortense laughs. "Talk to me in five years. Your mama and I were never getting married, either. You can see how that worked out."

"How do you know Jing isn't coming back?"

"It's a quarantine. People inside have been exposed."

"Not if there is no disease. Besides, what kind of a quarantine is it, if there are no doctors, no gloves, no masks?"

Aunt Hortense dabs at her mouth with her napkin. "How would you know what a quarantine is supposed to look like?"

"Papa wears protective clothing when he treats an infectious patient. I've seen it."

"Precisely why I don't want you going on calls with your father."

"But I love going with him."

"I know." Aunt Hortense sighs. Her face softens. "Very well. I'll put this off until your papa gets home. But do me a favor and keep this between you and me, all right? As far as Mr. Sweeting is concerned, I am interviewing."

"Thank you," I whisper, leaping up from the table. I'm about to hug Aunt Hortense.

"Elizabeth, did you ask to be excused?" she barks. I come to my senses in the nick of time.

When I get home from Miss Barstow's that afternoon, the coaches, buggies, carriages, motorcars, and bicycles begin to arrive at the mansion, bringing the guests for the newspaper luncheon. Only men work in Uncle Karl's newsroom. If there were a woman reporter, I could ask her why Uncle Karl got so mad when I brought up the monkey. Was he trying to pick a fight, or did the monkey really matter? I bet it has something to do with the newspaper wars.

When Uncle Karl's *Call* doesn't sell as well as Mr. Hearst's *Chronicle,* it puts Uncle Karl in a foul mood. Could "the monkey" be a code name for a man who gives them tips about stories? Maybe one of his reporters will tell me.

I need to go to that luncheon. But how?

I could borrow one of Maggy's uniforms and pretend to be a maid. But Uncle Karl or Nettie would recognize me. Even if they didn't, would any man answer a serious question posed by a serving girl?

I could hide behind a potted plant and hope to hear what I need. But what are the chances that the monkey will be discussed?

There is only one way I can think of: to go as myself.

I peer through a hole in the shrubbery and see the men in small groups, drinking glasses in hand. Nettie and her maids are serving canapés on silver trays. Uncle Karl is deep in conversation, an unlit cigar in one hand and a whisky glass in the other.

I walk boldly up the path. This is the Sweetings' garden. I'm not afraid.

"What do we have here?" A man with a huge mustache smiles.

"Karl has a daughter he never told us about?" asks a jolly man with a big red nose.

I smile, then give my best curtsy. "I'm Mr. Sweeting's niece, and I have a question for you."

Uncle Karl's voice rises above the din. "Why, Peanut, say hello to the boys. Boys, this is my niece, Elizabeth Kennedy."

"Hello." I wave, then curtsy again.

Uncle Karl is headed my way, his watch chain jangling. "What can I do for you, my dear?"

"I was just wondering"—I look around at the men watching me now—"if anybody knew about a monkey or a man named Monkey."

Several sets of eyes turn to Uncle Karl, who takes a bite out of the end of his cigar.

"Monkey Warren's dead," a thin man with a square head says.

"She's saying we're monkeys," a man with a big belly, striped trousers, and shoes half off his feet shouts. I know him. I met him when I went to Uncle Karl's office. His name is Peter.

All the men laugh. Uncle Karl's arm shoots around my shoulders as he tries to usher me into the house. "Lizzie, now, don't worry your pretty little head about this."

I duck out from under his arm and plant my feet. "I don't have a pretty little head."

The men roar at this.

"She doesn't have a pretty little head." Peter winks at Uncle Karl.

"I'd like to know what's happening," I demand.

Uncle Karl laughs. "Help me out here, boys."

"The monkeys are in the jungle," somebody offers.

Now a skinny man in a moleskin waistcoat hops around with his hands in his armpits. Everyone claps and hoots.

Behind me I hear a quiet voice. "Do they know what happened to that monkey?"

I turn to see a big man—about three hundred pounds, with thick spectacles set into his cheeks. He's talking to the man with the big mustache.

I'm about to corner him, but Uncle Karl is too fast. He slips his arm around me again. "They're just playing with you, Peanut. Come on now. No more foolishness. Your aunt will have my head if she finds you here."

"It's just one question," I plead.

"Elizabeth." Uncle Karl leans in. His voice is low and hard. "That's enough. Do not stick your nose where it doesn't belong."

A Hundred and One Rules

Do they know what happened to that monkey? I heard that man say it. I heard it with my own ears. What did he mean?

I'm so upset, it's hard to think straight. My pencil helps me clear my head.

The men tried to hide it.
Uncle Karl denied it.
But I heard the big man
Ask about a monkey plan.

I find the orange cat and attach the message, then wait, hoping the cord will come down. I need to talk to Noah, not just send him messages. Besides, he must be tired of peaches and salami. He needs something warm to eat.

Aunt Hortense is on the telephone in the drawing room, talking about parlor meetings and women getting the right to vote. Why is she on *our* phone? She spends most of the day at her house.

When she gets off, I stare at her. She sees the question in my eyes and turns away.

"I trust you'll keep my business to yourself," she says.

In his column, Uncle Karl has been poking fun at ladies who are trying to get the vote. Could Aunt Hortense be helping them?

Impossible.

Aunt Hortense rings for Maggy to carry her papers to the Sweeting house. I watch as Maggy follows her across the way. Aunt Hortense has been depending on Maggy more and more. Nettie doesn't like this. Yesterday, Nettie tracked dirt onto Maggy's clean floor and then scolded Maggy for it in front of Aunt Hortense.

With Aunt Hortense gone, Noah's cord comes down, and I head straight upstairs with my basket. In it are pancakes, a roast beef sandwich, jars of water, caramels from Ocean Beach, and the poem I wrote for him. I can't wait to show him his poem.

Noah's eyes light up when he sees me. "Tell me everything," he says as I settle into my usual chair.

I tell him about the monkey and Uncle Karl's party first. I hope he won't ask too many questions, because I don't have any answers. Do I tell him Uncle Karl said Jing wasn't in the quarantine? Should I say I had to convince Aunt Hortense not to interview for another cook? I dig in the basket for the candy.

When I hand it to him, he looks hard at me. How does he know I'm not telling him everything?

"Uncle Karl couldn't find him," I whisper.

His eyebrows rise like Jing's. "That doesn't mean he's not there. He's hiding something, Lizzie."

"What is he hiding?"

"He knows more than he's saying."

I think about Uncle Karl watching me in the yard as I unwrap a caramel. "What makes you say that?"

"Baba said Uncle Karl meets with the Six Companies sometimes. Baba translates."

"What are the meetings about?"

"I don't know."

"The monkey is important. If we figure out about the monkey, we'll know a lot more," I say.

I tell Noah about the Trotters' motorcar and Astral Dog and how I thought I was going to have to dance in front of everyone.

He chews his caramel thoughtfully. "You don't like dancing?"

"I'm not good at it."

"Do you practice?"

"Of course not. What a horrible thought."

"Do you have instructions on how to do these dances?" Noah asks. He unpacks the basket and places it on the shelf with the dishes.

"In my notebook."

"Bring them. We'll learn together." There comes that crazy, mischievous smile.

"You and me?" I ask.

My mind flashes on Aunt Hortense and what she'd do if she saw me dancing with a Chinese boy alone in our attic.

"Sure." He grins. "I've done the lion dance. And that's a lot harder."

"What's that?"

"I wear a lion costume, and my friend Pu is behind me—he's the back end of the lion, and I'm the front."

"I wouldn't want to be the back end."

"Neither does Pu. He says he only got that position because of his name."

"Poo!" I laugh. "Hey, I wrote you a poem." I unfold the page for him.

I have a friend in the attic
Who's kind of a book fanatic.
He can't make a sound,
Or else he'll be found,
Which is more than a bit problematic.

He smiles. "It's good. Can I have it?"

No one has ever asked to keep one of my poems. "Sure," I say.

"Miss Lizzie!" Maggy's voice wafts up from the second floor.

Noah's face falls. "You just got here!"

I grab his hand and squeeze it.

"Lizzie, please stay. It's been four days. I'm going crazy." He leans in and whispers, "Maybe I should go back."

"No! Then you'll be caught in the quarantine and I'll be trying to get both of you out."

Noah's shoulders slide down. He chews his cheek. "Come back as soon as you can."

I close his door and steal down the servants' stairs, with his words still in my ears. *Lizzie, please stay.*

"You have a visitor at the Sweetings'," Maggy tells me.

Oh no! Aunt Hortense has a hundred and one rules about visiting. I must say the right things, wear the right clothes, visit in the right room, and set my calling card on the correct tray.

I dive into the one dress Aunt Hortense approves of. It flaps on me without the proper petticoats.

I'm still buttoning as I rush across the way, leaping over a dead rat, its black eyes bulging. Orange Tom is at it again.

The drawing room has scarlet chairs and long curtains that puddle on the floor. Gold angels hold up glass sconces, and paintings of racehorses hang on every wall. I'm hardly ever in here. No one visits me.

"Elizabeth," Aunt Hortense purrs in her important-lady voice. "Do come in, dear."

Then I see, it's only the Trotters. What a relief! There's Gus, Gemma, and a pudgy lady in a blue hat with jeweled hatpins. All three have freckled skin and strawberry-blond hair.

"Lizzie." Mrs. Trotter's calling card is on a silver tray on Aunt Hortense's polished zebrawood table. "I'm delighted to meet you."

I bob awkwardly.

"Gus has asked that we visit." Mrs. Trotter smiles at Gus, who turns the color of a ripe tomato.

Gemma hides behind her fan.

"I, um, wanted to ask you to the La Jeunesse cotillion," Gus mumbles.

"Me?" I look around.

Gemma's fan slips down. She has a huge smile on her face. Did she put him up to this?

"Of course you, Elizabeth," Aunt Hortense chides.

"I'm just . . . Are you sure?" I whisper, my face as hot as a fire poker.

"Yes," Gus says.

Aunt Hortense eyes me. She picks up a diamond-studded nutcracker and splits a walnut with a loud crack. "Elizabeth is delighted. It is lovely of you to ask."

"It is lovely," I say, and steal a glance at Gus.

He almost smiles.

"He's a quiet one, but still waters run deep," Mrs. Trotter says, holding one gloved hand with the other.

"Or gather pond scum," Gemma whispers.

"Shush, Gemma," Gus mutters.

"Are you sure I can't get you some tea?" Aunt Hortense asks. "Biscuits? Scones? Our Yang Sun's pastries melt in your mouth. You know I stole him from the Poodle Dog."

Mrs. Trotter stands up. "Oh no, we really must be going. I'm afraid we've overstayed our welcome already."

"Not at all. I'm just sorry it took us so long to find Elizabeth."

"Lizzie, where were you?" Gemma whispers.

"I was . . . um, indisposed," I say.

"Elizabeth," Aunt Hortense barks. "Ladies do not speak of such things."

"I thought that was the polite way to say it."

Aunt Hortense smiles stiffly at Mrs. Trotter. "As you can see, Elizabeth is still working on her memoirs."

We follow them down the hall and out into the entryway, with its high ceiling and the electric chandelier bigger than the one in the Grand Opera House.

I stand and wave as the Trotters climb into their carriage.

When the mansion door closes, Aunt Hortense shoots me a look that would kill a small dog. "I will not have my niece acting like a milkmaid at La Jeunesse. Miss Barstow says she heard you discussing warts and boils the other day. It's coarse, Elizabeth. There's a time and place for such things, but the cotillion is not—"

"Do I have to go?" I ask. "Because I'm sure to embarrass you. It's better if I stay home."

Aunt Hortense crosses her arms. "You'll go, and you'll love every minute."

Noah in My Room

It's even more difficult to get away from Aunt Hortense now that she has made it her mission to get me fitted for a dress and jacket, petticoats, stockings, a corset, and dancing shoes. Not to mention teaching me how to drink without slurping and take tiny bites of everything. With her watching my every move, I can't take care of the horses. Ho has to do it.

Still, I manage to get the dance instructions onto the collar of Orange Tom, and after school Noah and I have our first lesson. When I sneak my basket of supplies up to Jing's room, Noah is waiting, his arms crossed. "It isn't that hard," he announces.

"Everyone's gone except Maggy. Maybe we should practice in my room. That way I can crank up the gramophone and we can hear the music."

Noah considers this. Then he nods slowly, deliberately.

A thrill shoots through me. Noah in my room!

"If I go down to your room, you have to swear you'll try."

"I do try, and everybody stares, and they make fun of me when I'm not there."

"How do you know what they do when you're not there?"

"I just do."

"But isn't Gemma your friend now?"

"I guess."

"You don't sound sure."

I shrug.

He considers this. "Fen pretends to be my friend so I will help him with his arithmetic."

"You're good with numbers."

"Of course."

"Of course," I say, and imitate his swagger.

He squints at me. "Why would I say I'm not good at something?"

"Girls are supposed to pretend they're lousy at everything."

"Maybe because they are."

"No!" I stamp my foot.

He laughs. "If you're good at something, you should say it."

"It's easier to do that if you're a boy."

"I'll take your word for it. Now let's work on the dancing. Where's Maggy?"

"She's doing the floors downstairs."

"That takes all afternoon?"

"The way Maggy waxes, it does. Our kitchen floor is shinier than the Sweetings', and Aunt Hortense has five maids to clean hers. If it's all clear, I'll whistle."

"Whistle? You don't whistle. You thunder down the stairs. You holler to Billy. You drop things in your room."

"I don't drop things."

"You're always banging something against the floor."

"My boots. I kick them off."

"Kick your boots off; then I'll know to come down. That will seem like you."

"Okay. I'll go check on Maggy." I grab the empty water pitchers and slip out the door and down the stairs. Maggy is on her hands and knees with a scrub brush. The soap smell stings my nose and makes my eyes water. After she scrubs the floor, she waxes it. She'll be busy for a good two hours.

Back in my room, I pull the shades down, unlace my boots, and kick them off. They fly against the wall with a satisfying *thunk.* Then I open the door and wait for Noah.

My ears strain to hear his footsteps. Even when I see him creep down the hall, I can't hear him.

He slips in. I close the door and slide the lock.

He's here! So real, it's as if I'd just imagined him before. He looks around my room, his eyes lighting on the windowsill.

"Baba gave these to you." He picks up a tiny chair Jing carved out of wood. "I helped him make this one. He said you don't feel like you fit in. He said he made you a chair so you would know there's always a place for you at the table."

I stare at him. I've always loved that little chair, but I didn't know that was why he'd given it to me.

Noah's face relaxes into a smile, and he bows, one hand behind his back.

He takes my arm, and my neck gets hot. His palm feels strange on my back, like the skin is too aware of his hand. I'm sweating where I hold him.

Together we muddle through a simple waltz step. Noah doesn't know how to do this any better than I do. I'm not the only one stepping on the wrong foot.

I'm taller than Noah, but even that isn't important here.

I'm wearing my ordinary clothes, but my skirt feels lighter.

My plan was to crank up the gramophone, but it's too dangerous. What if Aunt Hortense came home early? How would I explain the loud music?

So I hum. The longer we dance, the more it seems like there is music. I like the way his hand feels in mine. I like standing so near to him.

A barrel rolls across the cobblestones. Outside, the light has shifted. How long has it been?

"Lizzie?" Noah whispers. He looks at me hard, and then his eyes skitter away.

"What?"

"I can't stay up there alone much longer. Where is my father?"

We stop dancing. "I don't know, but I'll find him." My words seem full of hot air. I don't know what to do next.

He gazes at the blind. Then sighs. "Here, let me show you the lion dance." He crouches down and hops on one foot like an animal on the prowl. I mimic him. His head pops up, his hands like paws. I hop when he hops and stay still when he does.

I fall over, and we try not to laugh.

He jumps and leaps, his legs like springs.

Then Billy drives Juliet through the Sweeting entrance. Noah must get back to his room before Billy comes up.

I put one finger over my mouth; with the other I point upstairs. Noah nods, then tiptoes to the door. "Lizzie, you'll tell me if you find out something about Baba." His eyes shift.

"Of course! But I've told you everything I know."

"No matter what happens, you'll tell me?"

"Yes."

"Swear you won't tell anybody about me. Nobody. Ever. Swear it," he whispers.

"I haven't told anyone."

"I know that. Wait!" He takes a needle out of his sleeve and stabs his thumb with it. We watch the drop of blood appear, a bright spot of red on his brown skin.

I look into his eyes, dark eyes, true eyes . . . the eyes of a friend who knows more about me than anyone else.

"I swear."

I push my thumb toward him. He pokes it, one quick jab, glancing up as if he hopes he didn't hurt me. Our thumbs touch. Blood to blood.

CHAPTER 19

Chicken

Saturday morning, before I'm even out of my night-clothes, Nettie is in my room searing my scalp with a curling iron; then she twists combed whorls of my hair up tight, each pin like a weapon. I beg for Maggy, but Nettie says, "Fiddle-faddle. Maggy isn't a lady's maid. She doesn't know how to do hair. If Maggy worked in the Sweetings' household, she'd be a scullery maid."

When Nettie leaves, I rip out half of the hairpins and loosen the rest.

But Aunt Hortense loves my hair. All day she and Nettie hover, drilling me: Which fork do I use for dessert? Which is my water glass? My bread and butter plate? Then Nettie insists on giving me a manicure. Torture.

I can't get a moment to visit Noah. Luckily, I brought him extra food and water last night.

When it's finally time to get dressed, it takes me half an hour to get everything on, even with Maggy's help. The bodice of my dress has layers of white feathers. It fits so snugly, Maggy can barely get the dress fastened over my corset. She has to put my shoes on for me, because I can't lean over to hook them.

The shoes pinch. The dress is so tight, my ribs may crack. Will I be able to sit down? Will I leave a trail of chicken feathers wherever I go?

When I see myself in the mirror, my heart stops.

I look from the side. Straight on. From the back with a hand mirror. I run down to the bathroom to check that mirror, and the downstairs one, too.

I see me . . . but the prettiest me imaginable. I almost look like Hattie or one of the beautiful girls at Miss Barstow's. How could this be?

From one side of the room to the other I sashay, just to hear the swish of the dress on the floor, imagining what Gemma will say when she sees me. I peek in the mirror again. In my regular clothes I'm straight up and down. Now I have curves. It's almost worth the bother to look this way.

When Billy comes downstairs, he gapes at me, then whistles.

I glare at him. "It's nothing," I say, but his response shocks me. I really do look different.

When Aunt Hortense sees me, her eyes beam so brightly, I have to look away. "Oh, how I wish your papa were here to see this. You are looking more and more like your mother every day."

I should thank her, but the words won't come out. I let her hug me, then stomp out the back door, my face hot. I walk across to the Sweeting carriage house, which is like a palace, with electric lights and hot and cold running water and a carpet in the tack room. Tonight I'll be riding like a princess in a fine carriage.

Ho has the black carriage harnessed to four bay horses, each with four white socks. The horses have been bathed and groomed, and their coats are gleaming. Petting their sleek necks and soft muzzles makes me feel like myself again. Then I dust off my gloves. Can't go to La Jeunesse smelling like a horse.

I climb into the carriage. Ho picks up the lines, and the horses trot forward, four pairs of ears pricked.

We pick up Billy in front of our house. Even with a faint black eye, Billy is impressive in his Prince Albert cutaway and black gloves. Ho scoots over, and Billy slides in to command the team.

Uncle Karl and Aunt Hortense stand together in the driveway. Aunt Hortense's smile is radiant. I meet her eyes and smile, but I can't admit that I'm glad she went to all this trouble for me. Still, I think she knows.

"Is that our Peanut?" Uncle Karl asks Aunt Hortense.

"The very same," my aunt replies.

Billy waves goodbye, and the horses trot out the grand entrance, tails swishing, hooves clacking.

When we get to the Palace Hotel, the line is a block long, filled with the finest carriages, fringe-topped surreys, hacks, landaus, coaches, and buggies. A lone automobile waits in line, its motor spewing steam. Horses champ at their bits, paw the ground, spread their legs, and pee in the driveway. Silk-coated Chinese porters with velvet-handled shovels scurry about picking up green manure the second it drops to the ground.

Ho will return at eleven when the cotillion ends. Can I manage that long in this corset, making conversation about warts and excessive earwax with a boy I barely know? I'd like to see a young man tied into a corset for an evening. He'd never put up with it! Still, I can't wait to see Gemma and Hattie. What will they say about me?

We roll into the Palace courtyard, making a splendid show. At the front of the line, a man with a big stomach and a topper swings a jewel-handled cane as he announces our arrival. It's Peter, the man who works for Uncle Karl. He's got a deep voice perfect for announcing. Plus, he knows everyone. Somebody must have pegged him for this.

"And here we have the lovely coach of Mr. and Mrs. Karl Sweeting. Mr. William and Miss Elizabeth Kennedy . . . what an honor to ride in your uncle's finest."

"The coach gets better billing than we do," I whisper to Billy as I step out, barely avoiding tripping on my hem.

But Billy's attention is on a girl with a waist the circumference of a teacup, black hair, and a crimson dress. Everyone's watching her, but she doesn't seem to see them. Her face lights up when Billy takes her hand.

Then Gus appears in a cutaway with a boutonniere. His hands are shoved into his pockets, his shoulders hunched forward. His hair is newly cut, his shoes as shiny as polished spoons.

When he sees me, he smiles and stands up straight.

"Don't say anything. I know I look like a giant chicken," I tell him under my breath.

"Luckily, I like chicken," he mumbles.

I smile at him. His hands are still jammed into his pockets, but for a second I see the man he is becoming. My cheeks are hot as we walk together.

What do I say? Launching a discussion about earwax suddenly seems like a bad idea. "Where's Gemma?" I ask.

"She's supposed to be with Spencer, but he doesn't seem to know that."

"Oh no! He doesn't know he's Gemma's escort?"

Gus shrugs. "He knows."

"Let's go find her."

Gemma is wearing a painted silk dress with a blue beaded bodice that brings out the blue in her eyes. She's already seated at one of the long white tables ablaze with candles. When she sees me, her eyes glisten. "Lizzie! You look so pretty."

"You do, too," I say. "What happened to Spencer?"

Her nostrils flare. She looks away.

"Want us to go find him?"

She nods.

I follow Gus to the back of the enormous, glass-domed courtyard filled with palms. Light pours in from the glowing ceiling, and violins play. In the middle of the floor, Spencer dances with a beautiful blond girl in a dress the color of the evening sky. Spencer can't take his eyes off her.

"Spencer." I'm about to lurch forward and give him a

piece of my mind. How dare he dance with someone else when he came with Gemma?

Gus takes me by the hand, which stops me cold. Sweat drips down under my corset. "Do we have to dance?"

Gus smiles at me.

We stand at the edge of the dance floor full of glittering dresses and dark pressed suits. It smells of perfume and perspiration. Spencer and the girl in the evening-sky dress look as if they'll never come off the floor. If we're going to talk to him, we'll have to dance out there.

I close my eyes and pretend Gus is Noah and this grand courtyard is my cozy room at home.

Gus's hand is on the small of my back. His touch is lighter than Noah's. He's taller; we're eye to eye. Where do I look? Gus's steps are quick as he steers me over to Spencer. I'm a half beat behind him. He slows down; I speed up. Where are his feet? I barely miss stepping on them. My face gets hotter.

"Can I talk to you?" Gus murmers to Spencer.

Spencer tries to swing the evening-sky girl away.

Gus repeats his question, boldly.

Spencer frowns. "Now?"

"Yes." Gus cuts in. He takes the hand of Spencer's partner.

Oh no! *I* have to dance with Spencer? I stand stock-still as Gus and the girl dance away.

Spencer offers his hand to me, as if mine is covered in snot. He holds me with stiff arms so our bodies don't touch. His feet move in a square, his eye on the girl, his every move meant to say how irritated he is to dance with the likes of me.

I screw up my courage. "I thought you were here with Gemma."

"She's on crutches. How am I supposed to dance with her?" He swirls me closer to Gus.

"She can still dance."

He snorts.

"Why'd you ask her, then?"

"Our mothers arranged it," he says. He and Gus switch partners again.

A smile darts across Gus's lips as he takes my hand. He's happy to have me back! Maybe it wasn't Gemma's idea for him to ask me to La Jeunesse. Could it have been Gus's?

"I don't like Spencer," I say. Billy and the pretty dark-haired girl float by.

"He's full of himself."

"He said it wasn't his idea to ask Gemma."

"That's true. Gemma's always plotting. It backfired this time. I just hope she doesn't fall again. She's accident-prone when she gets upset."

A waiter in a white jacket announces, "Dinner is served."

We follow the flow of the crowd into the dining room. A band plays, and girls in sweeping dresses and boys in black jackets load their plates with oysters and creamed lobsters, sizzling soups and sourdough bread. Crab cakes and crumb-crust pies. Pork chops, pear tarts, and Parmesan potatoes. Bear meat and beef bourguignon. The tables of food go on and on.

We fill plates for ourselves and for Gemma, then join Hattie and her partner at Gemma's table. Spencer's hat and gloves sit on the chair next to Gemma, but that's all we see of him. With Hattie here, I stiffen. She says nothing about my dress, but her eyes judge me.

"Lizzie, I'm surprised to see you here," she says. "Have you ever even been to a cotillion dance before?"

"No," I say.

"Did you dance?"

"Yes."

"I'm so sorry I missed it." Hattie puts her lipstick in her tiny beaded purse.

I think about what Noah would do. He'd tell the truth. I look Hattie straight in the eye. "I'm not half the dancer you are, Hattie. None of us are. But I like dancing with Gus."

Gus turns bright red, and so do I. Why do I have to be so awkward? Still, it's true. And saying this makes Hattie back off. I can't wait to tell Noah.

I concentrate on my food, which I have been shoveling in. When my chest feels like a furnace packed with coal, I set my fork down and look around. That's when I notice Peter walk by.

"I'll be right back," I whisper to Gus, then charge after Peter as best I can in my long ruffly skirt and high heels. "Excuse me, sir?"

Peter ignores me.

"Sir . . . Peter," I practically shout, nearly tripping over a brocade-covered table.

He glances back. "Lizzie Kennedy, isn't it?"

"Yes, sir." I hurry to catch him. "I'm sorry I only know you by Peter."

"Indeed. What can I do for you, Miss Kennedy?" He's picked up speed.

"I want you to tell me the truth, sir." I scramble after him.

"The truth, is it?" He glances back. "Always a dangerous prospect."

"About the monkey."

"Ahh, yes. What, if I may ask, is your great interest in primates?" I'm trying my best to keep up.

"Well, sir, there's something going on with a monkey. People aren't talking about it, and I don't know why."

"Ah, my dear, there are many things people don't see fit to discuss. Surely you've learned that in your fourteen years."

"Thirteen."

"Even so."

Now I see that he's headed to the bar, where women aren't allowed. "You know what I want to know."

"My fair lady, you give me far more credit than I deserve."

I jump in front of him, trying to prevent him from going inside.

"Miss Kennedy, I'm sorry I can't be of more help. If you'll excuse me." He dips around me.

"Wait!" I shout.

He doesn't look back. He joins a crowded table, but I'm

stuck outside. Billy could follow him in there. It is annoying to be a girl sometimes.

The curls Nettie worked so hard on are falling into my face, so I blow them away.

Peter clinks his glass. "Gentlemen, your health," he toasts, slipping his shoes off under the table and settling in. I wave, hoping somebody will notice me, but no one looks my way.

CHAPTER 20

The Wolf Doctor

At Gemma's table everyone has moved on to dessert. Hattie is taking tiny bites of chocolate cake; Gemma is dipping her fork in raspberry filling. "You're up to something," Gemma whispers when I slip back into my chair.

Everyone stares at me.

"What makes you say that?" How I wish I could lie the way Billy does.

"Lizzie, you have to come with us. We can't dance without you," Hattie announces.

I look at Gus. He seems to know what I'm thinking.

"I'm still working on dessert," he tells her. I thank him with a smile.

When Hattie and her date are gone, I tell Gemma, "I want to talk to Peter—the man who announced us when we arrived. Only, now he's in the bar and he doesn't want to come out."

Gemma leans toward me, her eyes sparkling. "You want to go into the saloon?"

I nod.

"Let's go." She grins, scoots out of her seat, and grabs her crutches, with Gus close behind.

I'm starting to see that this is how Gemma and Gus are: Gemma gets bored and comes up with a wild idea, and Gus helps her pull it off. This time it's my idea.

Still, they didn't even ask me why I want to talk to Peter. It's important to me, so it's important to them. Is this what it means to have friends? How could I have missed Gemma at Miss Barstow's before? Are there other girls there as nice as she is?

We stop and look around outside the bar. A tea cart is tucked against the wall. Gus borrows a tablecloth from a nearby table and drapes it over the top.

Gemma yanks up the cloth. "Can you fit under this?"

I squat down to see if I can get my ruffles and feathers underneath. Luckily, they've loosened up since Maggy laced me in. I nod.

"Gus can push the tea cart," Gemma says.

"How are we going to explain pushing a tea cart in the bar?" I ask.

"I know," Gus says, and disappears. In a few minutes, he's back with a white waiter's jacket over his arm.

"Where'd you get that?" I ask.

He grins. "I've been here with Papa. I saw where they

keep them." He takes off his Prince Albert and hands it to Gemma, then slides his arms into the small waiter's jacket.

"Don't button it," Gemma says. She turns to me. "What will you do when you get in there?"

"I'm going to make that man Peter answer my question."

"How?"

How do you force someone to tell you something? Hmmm. Then I flash on his shoes. "By ransoming his shoes. He took them off."

Gemma bursts out laughing.

I crawl under the tea cart. Gemma figures out a way to fold the cloth back so I can peek through. She tucks in my skirt. Gus pushes the cart and leaves me behind.

"Not so fast," I whisper. "I can't keep up."

We practice until we get it. Then Gus maneuvers the tea cart over the doorway bump into the bar.

"Sir," Gus says when our cart is in line with Peter's table, "may I take your empties?"

Perfect. I'm liking Gus better and better. Peter doesn't notice Gus. A waiter is invisible to him. Is this why Jing doesn't want Noah working for anyone?

I lift up my tablecloth and the one on Peter's table and duck my hand under, trying to see the shoes in the dark tangle of legs. I manage to grab one shoe but brush a leg as I do. The leg jerks back. I freeze.

But no one calls out or peeks underneath. I crawl back under the tea cart, holding the shoe to my chest, then reach out and squeeze Gus's ankle.

Gus pretends to drop something and ducks his head under the cart. I nod vigorously, and he begins pushing the tea cart toward the door with all my ruffles underneath. I have all I can manage trying to hold the shoe and inch forward in this dress. I need both hands to crawl. I put the shoe under my armpit. That doesn't work. I hold the shoelace between my teeth. The shoe bonks my chest, flapping this way and that.

When we're safely over the doorway bump and around the corner, Gemma lifts the table skirt, and I hop out.

Gus and Gemma burst out laughing when they see the shoelace in my mouth.

"Good job, Lizzie." Gemma straightens my dress and smoothes my hair.

We wait for Peter to discover that his shoe is missing. But Peter is busy toasting his buddies and knocking back shots. Gemma goes in search of more dessert. Finally Gus and I see Peter wiggle around in his seat, then duck under the table.

Gus grins. I put my hands over our mouths so we won't laugh out loud.

"I'll tell him you have it," Gus says, and marches in wearing his own jacket. He whispers into Peter's ear.

Peter's head swivels in my direction. He stomps out, one shoe on, one shoe off.

His breath stinks of whisky. His jacket is off. A perspiration stain marks his white shirt. He glares. "I do not appreciate your high jinks, Miss Kennedy. Why have you chosen me to persecute?"

"You know what I need to know, sir."

He groans. "Is this about the monkey?"

"Yes, sir. I'm sorry to bother you, but it's very important."

He sighs. "Dr. Kinyoun, a misguided physician with an inflated view of his own worth, believes he has conclusive evidence that the plague has come to our city. He claims to have proven this by injecting the plague pathogen, supposedly culled from a dead man, into a rat, two guinea pigs, and a monkey. The rat and the guinea pigs died. We're waiting to see if the monkey survives."

"That would prove the plague is here?"

"That's the claim of Dr. Kinyoun—also known as the wolf doctor."

"Why is this a secret?"

"It isn't, exactly. Your uncle is opposed to giving ink to such shenanigans. We leave that sort of scurrilous reporting to Hearst's *Examiner*. Now, my shoe, please."

"And what about the quarantine?"

"The dead man who allegedly had the plague was found in Chinatown. The wolf doctor called the quarantine, and now he's trying to prove to everyone it wasn't a mistake."

"Will you tell me if the monkey dies? Please, sir?"

"*Will I tell you?* Miss Kennedy, I have indulged you beyond what any prudent gentleman would, could, or should. Now, shall I get word to your aunt and uncle of your behavior, or will you kindly return my property to me and let this be the end of it?"

I hand over his shoe. "Thank you, sir." I bob my head.

When I turn around, Gus is standing by the table taking this all in. Gemma is hobbling along on one crutch, holding a plate piled high with cookies.

"You did it!" Gemma offers me a cookie.

"With your help. What a team you two are!"

Slowly, we drift to the courtyard to wait for our coaches, letting others go in front of us. None of us wants to leave.

When I get home, Maggy and the parrot are waiting up for me. "Miss Lizzie, have fun?" Maggy asks.

"Yes, actually," I say, thinking how I must remember every detail to tell Noah.

In my room, she unlaces the corset. The stays and ties have left red impressions on my skin. It feels wonderful to be out of it. I pull on my soft flannel nightdress and crawl into bed. Maggy turns out the gas lamp. Only the moon's light remains.

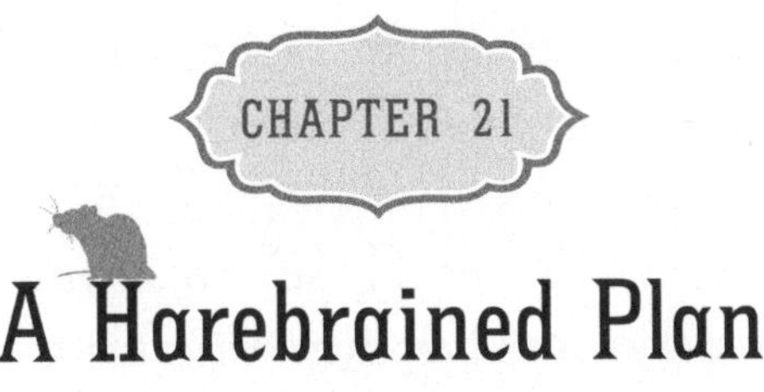

CHAPTER 21

A Harebrained Plan

When I wake up the next morning, I think about what Peter said. The entire quarantine rides on a monkey? How can that be true? What will happen if the monkey dies? Will they make it a real quarantine, with doctors and nurses and yellow plague flags? Why isn't it a real quarantine now?

All I have is questions. I want to go back to Noah with answers. I take out the feather Nettie wove into my hair. I was so tired last night, I fell asleep with it in.

My eyes find Jing's gifts. I've been out having fun in my white-feathered dress while Jing has been locked in Chinatown. Why is it I've never given Jing a gift? I don't even know when his birthday is. I have to get him out of there, and I'm not going to wait around for a stupid monkey.

I'm still trying to figure out a plan when Billy knocks on my door.

"C'mon," he says. "I need to teach you something. Now, before church and before everyone gets up."

I stare at him, not moving from where I'm curled up in my quilt. It's been so long since Billy taught me anything.

"You may not realize this"—his face turns red—"but you're . . . All dressed up last night, you . . . Look, you need to know how to defend yourself."

"Against what?"

"People. Men. The world isn't what you think." He frowns. "Put on your old clothes. Meet me at the barn."

He shuts the door, and I slip into an old skirt. When I get down to the stable, Billy has his boxing gloves on. He's practicing punching the air. He sees me and stops.

"Okay. Let's say it's dark and you're walking in from the barn, and someone comes at you like this." He lunges for me. "What would you do?"

"Kick him in his reproductive apparatus?"

"Not a bad idea. But what happens if he has you like this?" He stands behind me, his arm around my throat.

I shake my head. Or try to, anyway. I can hardly move with my neck in the vise of his arm.

"I'm going to keep it simple, and then we're going to practice. Did Papa ever explain to you how to defend yourself?"

"No."

"Of course not." He snorts. "Look, you should never do this if you're kidding around, but if you're in danger . . . there are points on a person, Lizzie, that will kill them. Temple, armpit, liver, groin. Behind the ear."

He spends an hour making me practice different moves until I have mastered them. It's so nice to have the old Billy back. He could be instructing me on how to dig for turnips and I'd be happy.

The next morning after Maggy comes down, I sneak up and leave Noah supplies on the bottom step. He knows to watch for them now.

I want so badly to go up and see him. Maybe later the cord will be down. Maybe I will have found Jing by then. Wasn't Papa supposed to be back by now?

I gather clean towels, cloths, bandages, gauze, Papa's contagion gloves, a mask, and a medical coat. I roll them into a tight ball and put them in the bottom of my book bag. The bag is overstuffed, which Aunt Hortense is sure to notice. I head down the long path to the Sweetings' stable. If I climb into the carriage here, Aunt Hortense won't see my bag.

Ho is in the back, shining bits. "Excuse me, Ho," I say. "I need to go to school."

Ho jumps. "Yes, miss." He hurries to the black horses already harnessed to the buggy.

Aunt Hortense comes out when she sees us. She peeks into the carriage. "Eager to get to school, are we?"

"Yes, ma'am," I say.

"Happier at Miss Barstow's, I take it?"

All along Aunt Hortense has said I would grow to like Miss Barstow's. I can't admit she's right. I don't meet her eyes.

"Glad to hear it. Have a good day." She taps the carriage, and Ho drives on.

All during school, I can barely concentrate. After elocution, Hattie brings up Spencer.

"Spencer? Spencer who?" Gemma sniffs. "But *you-know-who* is totally smitten."

"I noticed that," Hattie says, and waggles her eyebrows at me. "The question is . . . how does Lizzie feel about him?"

Hattie and Gemma look at me.

"Gus? Of course I like Gus," I say.

They nod, waiting for more.

"I had fun, okay?"

"That's it?" Gemma asks. "That's all we're going to get?"

"Yes." I hurry down the front steps in such a fluster, I forget to check my slip. There are mirrors hung everywhere because Miss Barstow can't stand it when your slip is showing. "Lizzie, a penny, please." Miss Barstow holds out the orphan jar. I fork over a penny. You have to contribute every time she catches you with your petticoat hanging. The money goes to the McKinley Orphanage.

I run back inside to fix my slip.

"What's the matter with you today?" Gemma whispers as we gather our books.

"Nothing."

"I don't believe you," she announces.

If only she and Gus could help me with this. If only

I could tell her about Jing. But it's one thing to play a ransom game with a shoe, another thing to sneak into the quarantine zone of Chinatown.

When Ho comes after school, I dive into the carriage.

"Um, Ho." I clear my throat to control the trembling. "Could you take me to a friend's house?"

"Yes, miss. Where is that?"

I hold my breath. "Down by Chinatown."

Ho's Adam's apple slides up and down. He steals a look back. "Mrs. Sweeting knows about this?"

"Of course." I try to sound convincing, but mostly I'm just loud.

I've put him in a bind. He doesn't want to displease me, as I can report him to Aunt Hortense. But if he goes along with what Aunt Hortense calls "Elizabeth's harebrained plans," she'll have his head.

I watch which way he steers the horses. Toward home or Chinatown? I hold my breath.

Chinatown!

We're getting close. I can see the barricade up ahead. Ho fidgets, stealing glances back at me.

I spot a nearby building with paint peeling from the posts, blinds down and one boarded up window. "Here," I say.

He pulls the horses up. "Miss? I don't think—"

I jump out of the carriage. "Tell Aunt Hortense I'll be home before dark."

"Miss, are you sure Mrs. Sweeting—"

"Yes, yes. She knows." I slip around a corner and wait.

When he's gone, I tie on the protective mask, the cap,

the coat, and the gloves. For once, I'm glad I'm tall. With the mask on, I can pass for an adult.

Papa says there are woman doctors, but since I've never seen one, I'm going to pretend to be a nurse. It would be better if I had a proper uniform underneath the medical coat, but no matter. I head to the quarantine zone. My hands sweat in the gloves. I untie the bottom of the mask so I can breathe.

Here the quarantine line is nothing more than a wire across the road. Surely I can get through that.

Two policemen patrol the wire. "Excuse me! Excuse me, sir!" I wave. "I have to get inside. I have to see patients."

"What? Who are you?" the tall policeman with shiny buttons asks. The other policeman is eating a sandwich.

"I'm Dr. Kennedy's assistant," I say.

"Who's he? What you got all that on for?"

"In case of contagion, sir."

The tall policeman steps closer. He looks me up and down. "How old are you?"

"Twenty-two," I lie.

"Twenty-two?" He snorts. "How old are you really?"

"Twenty-one," I try again.

He laughs. "Lost a year already. Don't you know it's a crime to lie to a police officer? Ben, how old you think this one is?"

The other officer squints at me.

"Take the mask off," the first officer says.

I untie it.

He shakes his head. "Even younger than I thought. Fourteen at most. That right?"

A drop of sweat slips down beneath my shirtwaist.

The policeman crosses his stiff arms. "You don't have any business in there."

I stand stupidly, unsure if I should keep pretending or tell the truth.

The policeman turns away. "Ben, you got another one of them sandwiches?"

Now what? Maybe I can try again on the other side of the quarantine area. I'm marching that way when I hear the wheels of a carriage creak behind me.

Gemma's head pops out. "Lizzie! Lizzie, is that you?"

The Trotters! Gus, Gemma, and their driver.

"What in the world are you doing?" Gemma demands as their carriage pulls up beside me.

"What am *I* doing?"

Gus and Gemma exchange a look. "You were acting weird at school," Gemma explains. "We decided to follow you. And it's a good thing we did."

"I was not acting weird," I say.

"You were. Why are you dressed like that?"

"Our cook, Jing, is stuck in the quarantine. I'm trying to get him out."

"Quarantine for what?" Gemma asks.

"The plague," Gus tells her.

"For goodness' sake, Lizzie, take that stuff off and get into this carriage right now." Gemma pats the seat next to her.

I look over at the policeman patrolling. I didn't fool this one. What makes me think I'll fool the next? Will they take me to the police station next time? Put me in jail? No telling what Aunt Hortense will do if she has to bail me out.

I climb up into the Trotter carriage.

Gemma helps me get the mask untied. "If your cook has been in the quarantine, he'll be contagious."

"It's not a real plague outbreak," I say.

"Why else would they have a quarantine?" she asks.

"It has to do with a monkey," Gus explains. "We're waiting to see if a monkey dies. And if the monkey dies, it might really be the plague."

"That is the craziest thing I've ever heard," Gemma tells me.

"I know, but it's true."

"Why is Jing so important?" Gemma asks as I settle in between Gemma and Gus.

"He's our cook. He's a member of our family," I say as we pass a row of run-down buildings. Laundry hangs out the window to dry. Pigeons coo and scurry around buckets of old crab shells, the air thick with the smell of fish.

Gus nods, his brow furrowed. "Wouldn't it be better to try to get him out than try to get you in?"

"I just . . . haven't been able to figure out how."

"We'll help you." Gus smiles at me.

I look from Gus to Gemma. They actually seem excited to be a part of this. Did anyone ever have better friends than these two?

The Trotters live in a yellow house with a witch's cap turret and big bay windows that look clear down to the bay and the little island of Alcatraz. The Trotters' garden is filled with yellow, pink, peach, and lavender roses. Mrs. Trotter is on the porch with a big floppy hat and pruning shears.

Gemma takes me up to her room. It's larger than mine, with pale yellow striped wallpaper, a wicker back rocker, a hat stand filled with hats, and a table jammed with music boxes.

When Gus comes in, he has a pen, paper, and an envelope. He sits down at Gemma's writing desk.

"What are you up to?" Gemma wants to know.

"Writing a letter."

I glance over at the stationery: TROTTER, BLACK, AND JESSUP, ATTORNEYS AT LAW.

"On Papa's letterhead?" Gemma asks.

"Yep," he mutters.

We watch as Gus dunks the pen into the ink, taps off the excess, and begins writing. Gemma leans over his shoulder.

"It has come to my attention," Gemma reads, *"that the cook in the residence of the esteemed and revered Dr. Kennedy has been unable to see to his duties. Dr. Kennedy's work has been impeded by his cook's absence. His absence has caused heartache and hardship of great magnitude for the Kennedys, and it is important, imperative, and essential that he be released at once. . . ."*

Gemma's mouth drops open. "You're not going to sign Papa's name."

"Course not." Gus smiles a sly smile. "I'm going to sign my name."

"Gus! He was named after Papa," she tells me. "Still"—

she raises her eyebrows at him—"he won't like you using his stationery."

They stare at each other, considering this.

"It's pretty good, though. Official, like the way he writes," Gemma says.

Gus's eyes are on me. Is it my opinion that matters to him?

"Sounds like a lawyer to me," I say.

"And it's for a good cause. You know how Papa always talks about making moral decisions," Gemma says, nodding now.

Gus bends his head over the page, his pen nib scratching against the paper as he finishes his letter.

There's a hop to my step as I climb up into the Trotters' carriage.

We don't want to risk running into the same policemen I talked to earlier. So we take a long route around to the other side of Chinatown.

Beyond the ropes and sawhorses of the quarantine line, red lanterns hang, carved wooden dragons wind around a pole, and red silk shirts flutter in the breeze. I search the faces as I always do, but no Jing.

Gus presents the envelope to a mounted policeman, who reads the letter, rubs his eyes under his spectacles, and reads it again. The policeman refolds the letter and slips it back into the envelope. "Sorry, son." He returns the letter to Gus. "I'm afraid I can't do that."

"But we need our cook," I say.

The policeman shrugs. "You, me, and my aunt Theresa. We let them all out, won't be much of a quarantine, now, will it?"

"But that's a letter from a lawyer," Gemma points out.

"I see that, miss, but it isn't a court order. I'm sorry. I can't let you through. Go on now." He flaps his hand. "We need to keep this area free of traffic."

The Trotters' driver turns the carriage around. I look back at the paper parasols and cone-shaped bamboo hats hanging on hooks. On this side, the signs are all in English.

Gemma takes my hand and squeezes it. "Sorry, Lizzie."

No one says anything else the rest of the way home. I begin to wonder if I'm ever going to get Jing out.

CHAPTER 22

Button-Head Lion

After school the next day, the cord is down. I take the stairs two at a time. But then I remember that Noah will need supplies, and I run back to the kitchen to fill my basket.

When Noah opens the door, I fill him in on everything in a big rush. I explain what Peter said and how I tried to pretend to be a nurse to get into Chinatown. I tell him how Gus Trotter wrote a letter on his father's letterhead, but that didn't work, either.

His upper lip trembles. "You're going to give up, aren't you?" he whispers.

"Of course not," I say.

He flashes his crazy grin. "I wish I could go with you."

I think about how nice it would be for Noah and me to walk down the street, or ride in the carriage, or bicycle in

Golden Gate Park like other friends do. "I wish you could, too."

"Hey." He smiles. "I made something for you." He pulls a small brown paper-wrapped package out of his pants pocket and hands it to me.

I unfold the paper and pull out a piece of fabric. A buttonhole strip. Except mine has a button in the buttonhole. The button is the head of an animal, the body is sewn in gold thread. It has four big paws and a tail with a yellow puff at the bottom. Around the button a thick yellow mane has been fluffed out from the strip. Noah has made me a button-head lion.

"So you'll remember to be brave," he says.

"With the girls at Miss Barstow's?" I ask.

"With everyone. Be your best true self. That's what Baba says."

I sigh. "That's hard."

"It takes a lot of courage," he agrees. "That's what I think about when I do the lion dance."

"Thank you for this," I whisper, holding the button against my chest.

He nods, pleased that I'm pleased.

"Lizzie!" I hear Billy tromping below.

Noah's face falls.

"Oh no," I whisper.

"LIZZIEEEE! Where the heck are you?"

I take off out of Jing's room and down the stairs. On the second floor, Billy sees me come out of the servants' stairwell.

"What were you doing up there?"

"Looking for the kittens."

"Kittens, huh?" He watches me closely. "What's the matter with you, anyway? This morning you were moping around like your horse died."

"I tried to get Jing out again. Didn't work."

Billy scratches his eyebrow and frowns. "I thought he'd have found a way home by now. Maybe he needs our help."

"Of course he does. What do you think I've been telling you!"

He shrugs, stares out the hall window. "There's this woman, Donaldina Cameron, who lives in Chinatown with a bunch of girls. If there's a girl in trouble, she rescues them. People call her the Angry Angel, because she gets people out of dangerous places. Anyway, I heard that her front door isn't quarantined. Her back door is."

"That doesn't make sense."

"What about this quarantine makes sense?"

"Nothing," I admit, sitting on the hall chair and unlacing my boots.

"I helped her get a girl out once. Climbed a tree, jumped in the window, and carried the girl down. She owes me."

"Out of where?"

"A bad situation." He picks a flower out of the hall vase and rips it apart petal by petal. "She was working for people in Presidio Heights. They were beating her."

"Why?"

He shrugs. "Bad people do bad things."

"She's okay now, right?"

He nods, wadding up the petals in his hand.

"You should tell Papa when you do things like that. It would make him proud."

"Which is exactly why I don't."

I frown at him. "Why wouldn't you tell him something that would make him happy?"

He sighs. "Because I don't want to do things *for him.* I want to do them *for me.*" He opens his hand.

"But you did it for you. What's the matter with just telling him?"

He snorts. "Put your shoes back on. You want to try this or not?"

I shove my toes back into my boots. "Of course I do. But what will we tell Aunt Hortense?"

He smiles in his sly Billy way. "Leave that to me."

"I understand you and William would like to go to the opera tonight," Aunt Hortense announces when I come down the stairs.

"Oh, yes," I say. *Opera?* I mouth the word to Billy behind Aunt Hortense's back.

He nods. Later, in the wagon, he explains. "We need time. The opera gets out late."

"She believed you."

"Of course. She believes everything I say."

"Must be nice."

"It is."

"But what happens when she comes home and we're not there?"

"She's going to a masquerade ball with Uncle Karl. We'll be home before she is," Billy says, and picks up the lines.

"Shouldn't we be wearing opera clothes?"

"She's upstairs. She can't see us."

"Won't Ho tell her?"

"No."

"Why not?"

"He owes me."

"Does everybody owe you?"

"Yes." He smiles. "As a matter of fact, they do."

We take the fast route to Chinatown and then go around to the back side. Through the quarantine wire, I see a vegetable stand, a few weird-looking bumpy green vegetables. Bins of brown roots. Not much there. Are they running out of food?

At the far corner, outside the wire, we stop at a plain three-story brick building. I can't see the back door from here, but there's the quarantine rope down the street.

"Why would they quarantine her back door but not her front door?" I ask.

"People think God will protect her because she's doing his work. Look, you stay here with John Henry." He climbs down. "I'll go in and talk to her."

The sun is setting, leaving an orange glow on the street. A group of Chinese girls in shirtwaists and skirts hurries up the front steps. A horse trots down the hill behind us. I'm getting a little more used to Chinatown, but still it is strange and I don't like sitting out here by myself. Although, technically I'm not in the quarantine, so this isn't Chinatown.

The darker it gets, the more anxious I become. I sit up tall, try to look fierce. But my feet are cold and my bottom is tired of sitting. Every time I see someone walk by, I jump. I think about Noah's lion. Being brave is a lot easier in daylight. Finally Billy comes out. "They're going to send someone in for him."

"What time is it?"

"Seven-thirty."

"What time is Aunt Hortense getting back?"

"Late. Those masquerade balls start late and last a long time."

"What if she calls the police?"

"What if she does? Do you want to get Jing out or not?"

The lights are on in Miss Cameron's house. A girl carrying a lantern walks by the window. Upstairs we hear girls singing.

"Billy?"

"Yes."

I pull my knees up. "Are you going to become a doctor?"

"No."

"Why not?"

"Remember when Mama died? Remember how sure Papa was that he could save her?"

"That wasn't his fault. He tried his best." I pull my coat tighter around myself.

"I know he did. That's why it's a stupid profession. Nothing he did worked."

"You can't prevent people from dying."

John Henry shuffles his legs. He bites at his shoulder, leaving a wet spit mark.

"But you shouldn't tell people you can help them when you can't," Billy says.

"It makes them feel better."

"It's a lie."

"But, Billy, sometimes you can help them."

"Yeah . . . I guess."

We listen to the distant foghorn and watch the fog roll in. Under a dim gaslight in Chinatown, a group of men in black are serving food to a long line of people. The smell of soy sauce wafts toward us.

A crucifix hangs in the window of Miss Cameron's house, backlit and eerie in the night. The singing has stopped. A girl giggles. Voices rise and fall, some in Chinese, some in English.

"So, what are you going to do?"

"Haven't decided. Might want to be a fighter," Billy says finally.

"Why?"

An owl hoots in the distance. A family of raccoons scurries down the street, making their strange clicking sounds. "It's fun."

"It's fun to get a black eye?"

He shrugs. "I don't mind. Besides, there's a lot more to it than that."

I rearrange myself. Try to get comfortable. Use my purse as a pillow. I'm almost asleep when the wagon jiggles. I grab Billy's arm. "Billy!"

"Shush, Lizzie. It's okay," Billy whispers.

I turn back. A Chinese woman in a large silk tunic and silk pants and a red silken hat climbs into our wagon.

I tighten my hold on Billy's sleeve. "Billy!"

And then I see her face.

"Jing!" I dive over the seat to give him a hug. His face looks thinner. More drawn. And silly with that hat. "I can't believe it's you! Are you okay? What happened?"

"You two got me out." His voice has a tremble in it, but his lips are smiling. "Good trick."

"How did you get stuck in there? Do you know how worried we've been?"

"Shush, Lizzie!" Billy's eyes are on two policemen walking our way. Jing slinks down, crawls under an old saddle blanket.

On the way home, I keep glancing back at the blanket-covered lump. I don't want to let Jing out of my sight. I want to tell him everything that happened. How hard I tried to get him out. How strange it was to realize he had a son. I want to tell him about Gemma and Gus and how Miss Barstow's isn't so bad anymore. I want to ask him what he knows about Uncle Karl, and whether Jing is his last name or his first name. And why he gets mad at Noah but he never gets mad at me. There are a million things to ask, but mostly I want to tell him how much he means to me. How I didn't realize that, until now.

"Jing," I whisper to the saddle blanket, "when is your birthday?"

"Shush, Lizzie," Billy whispers.

"August 16," Jing whispers back.

As soon as we cross under the Sweetings' archway, we see that the light is on in our kitchen.

"Aunt Hortense?" I say to Billy.

"What time is it, anyway? I thought she'd still be out."

"What are we going to tell her?" I ask as she bursts out the door, still wearing her green masquerade dress, her Bible in her hand.

"I'll think of something," Billy mutters.

Jing peeks out from under the blanket.

"Thank God," she whispers as she reaches us.

"We're sorry to have worried you, Aunt Hortense." Billy's voice sounds sincere. He could actually be sorry he worried her. "But we got Jing."

"I see that. Good to see you, Jing."

Her hands are trembling. "Go inside. Both of you. We'll talk about this tomorrow." Her voice is hoarse. "But you should know that Mr. Sweeting has heard from your father. He'll be home late tonight. And of course you know that the quarantine is over."

Billy and I look at each other.

"You didn't know," she says. "So how did you get Jing . . . Oh, don't even tell me." She sighs. "I don't want to know."

CHAPTER 23

The Empty Room

The sun is rising when I wake up. Down in the kitchen, I hear the pop and hiss of bacon frying in the pan.

Jing is manning the skillet. Papa is reading the paper. There are baskets of biscuits on the table.

Everything is the way it's supposed to be.

"Lizzie!" Papa jumps up, wraps his long arms around me, and gives me a great big Papa hug.

"You were away too long. Don't do that again!"

"Couldn't be helped." He pushes my hair out of my face. "I missed you."

"I missed you, too, Papa." I beam at Papa and Jing. I can't wait to see Noah's face. He must be so happy to have his Baba back.

"I gave Jing an examination. As fit as a fiddle, of course. What a ridiculous charade that was."

I hold my breath, waiting for more. How does he think Jing got out? Aunt Hortense must have told Papa about last night.

Papa spreads jam on a biscuit. His face is relaxed, happy. Not twisted and small the way it gets when he's mad. Maybe she didn't tell him. "What happened while I was gone?" he asks.

I stick to safe subjects. I tell Papa and Jing about Gemma and Gus and La Jeunesse and how Miss Barstow's isn't so bad now that Gemma and I are friends.

Papa seems pleased.

My eyes fly to Jing, who knows more than anyone else about how hard Miss Barstow's has been for me. He saw how I always stood by myself. He tried to cheer me up when I came home miserable day after day.

"I would have liked to see you all dressed up," Papa says. "Aunt Hortense must have been beside herself." He pushes his glasses up his nose and taps the newspaper page.

"So glad that quarantine is over. But you?" Papa smiles at me. "You've got better things to worry about, like the next cotillion, I suppose."

I can't stand to have Papa think this. I'm about to open my mouth and tell him how untrue it is, when Jing steps over to offer me a biscuit. His eyes catch mine. He winks. I take a deep breath and manage to control my tongue.

"So." Papa looks at me. "Tell me more about this Gus fellow."

Even as I chatter, a sudden heaviness comes over me. The quarantine is over. What will happen to Noah now?

He'll go back to Chinatown. Will I be able to see him again? Can we visit each other? I don't want to lose him. He is my best friend. I like Gus and Gemma a lot, but I can't tell them everything the way I can with Noah.

After breakfast, Aunt Hortense's houseboys come and collect her things.

I try to sneak up the back stairs so I won't run into her, but she comes looking for me. "Elizabeth!" She follows me into my room. "You and I need to talk."

"I have to get ready for school," I say.

She plants her feet smack in front of me, poking at the hair neatly piled on her head. "We need to talk now."

Neither of us sits down.

"How did you get Jing out?"

"Donaldina Cameron got him out."

"Who is she?"

"Someone Billy knows." I don't look her in the eye.

"So that opera nonsense?"

"Billy said it wasn't exactly a lie, because we went by the opera."

She crosses her arms and stares at me. "What do you think?"

"It was a lie," I admit. "But why are you tougher on me than on Billy?"

"Between your papa and Mr. Sweeting, Billy has enough eyes on him. And that's beside the point here."

"Yes, ma'am."

"I'm glad Jing's back. I missed him, too. But you can't take matters into your own hands like that, Elizabeth, and then lie through your teeth to me. You can't treat me as if I'm nothing more than an obstacle for you to get around."

"Yes, ma'am."

"Don't 'yes, ma'am' me. Just tell me you didn't go to Chinatown."

"I didn't go to Chinatown," I say. Technically I didn't go, technically it isn't a lie, but . . .

"How exactly did you get him back?"

I stare at my quilt. "Like I said, this Donaldina woman got him back. She owed Billy."

Aunt Hortense nods. This is the way Uncle Karl does things. She's used to it.

"I'm sorry, Aunt Hortense," I whisper.

"I can't do this anymore, Elizabeth," she shakes her head.

"Are you going to tell Papa?"

"It's not your papa I'm worried about. It's you and me. Do you think we can ever learn to trust each other?"

What a question. I've never really thought about working something out with Aunt Hortense. Do I even want to? Not really.

I don't say this, but Aunt Hortense seems to know it anyway. She sighs, closes her eyes. Her lip trembles.

"Just remember there's a price to pay for secrets. Trust is what holds us together, Lizzie. Secrets tear us apart."

"You called me Lizzie," I whisper.

"So I did." Her hands are on the dresses in my closet, separating them so they hang an inch apart. When she gets to the end of the dresses, she leaves without another word.

* * *

When I get home from school, Uncle Karl and Papa are standing in the driveway talking. Papa has his arms crossed in front of him. Is Uncle Karl telling Papa about how I showed up at his newspaper luncheon?

I drift closer.

"I don't see it that way," Uncle Karl says.

Papa breathes in sharply. His face is red.

"Let him go, Jules." Uncle Karl brushes the ground with his foot. "Billy has to work this out for himself. You know he does." He glances at me. "And as for you, Peanut . . . I don't even know what to say about you."

Uncle Karl's intense blue eyes burn through me. I hold my breath, waiting for him to tell Papa what I did.

"So far as I can see, your daughter is going kicking and screaming into adulthood. Isn't that right, darlin'?" Uncle Karl asks.

I don't answer.

"You should have seen her all dressed up for La Jeunesse. You would not have recognized her." Uncle Karl is smiling, but his eyes are talking to me. He wants to make sure I know he's telling Papa only the good things.

I run around to see if the cord is down, careful to watch to make sure Uncle Karl doesn't see me.

It isn't. Too many people around. Where is Orange Tom? I check all of his usual haunts, including the new one in the bottom of the laundry chute.

Orange Tom has vanished.

All afternoon, I keep watch, but no matter where Papa,

Billy, and Maggy are, the cord does not come down. As for Jing, does he know I know about his son? Noah made me swear not to tell anyone. That includes Jing, doesn't it?

Why didn't I talk to Noah about this before? We only thought about getting Jing out, not what would happen after the quarantine ended and Jing came home.

It's early evening by the time Billy goes out, Papa walks across to the Sweeting house, and Jing goes to the barn to talk to the blacksmith. Maggy and the parrot take the laundry in.

But still no cord. I break Noah's rule and sneak up to the third floor.

Jing's door is closed.

"Noah?" I whisper.

No response.

"Noah?"

Still nothing. I take a deep breath and pull open Jing's door.

Noah's books are not piled on the chair. Noah's button strips aren't heaped on the bed. Noah's homework assignments aren't stacked on the bookshelf. The colorful thread balls Noah and the cat played with are gone.

The quarantine is over. Noah has gone back to Chinatown. It was only a matter of time before Papa and the Sweetings found him. It was no kind of life hidden in an attic room. It's better for Noah. It's better for Jing. It's better.

I run down to my room and slam the door and then I start to cry.

PART TWO

The Egg Trick

When I wake up, the first thing I think is no school for five whole days. It will take that long for Miss Barstow to move the school to the fancier spot in Presidio Heights. I stretch and yawn.

But then there's shouting in the hall. I run out. Billy's door is closed, but the voices come through it.

"You've been lying all this time?" Papa asks.

"Not lying, just not saying," Billy replies.

"Lies of omission are still lies."

"I didn't plan it. It just happened."

"It just *happened*? A successful person has a plan. No plan is a plan to fail."

"Failure, then. That's my choice."

"Don't be stupid, Billy," Papa snaps.

"You define 'stupid' as any decision you wouldn't make."

Jing comes up the stairs. He crosses his arms and rocks from foot to foot.

"Billy." Papa's voice softens. "Explain this to me in a way I can understand. You're earning money for a motorcar?"

"It's not just that. I like to fight."

"That is a barbaric sensibility."

"Uncle Karl doesn't think so."

"Uncle Karl and I don't see eye to eye on most subjects. You know that."

"He knows more than you do about how to stand up for yourself. People take advantage of you."

"They do not."

"Remember that time in San Mateo? They said they didn't send for the local doctor because they knew he'd charge and you would treat them for free."

"Yes, I remember. And I never went back."

"I don't want people to take advantage of me. I need to be able to back up what I say. Otherwise it's just talk."

"Courage comes from your heart, not your fists."

"People don't push you around if you can handle yourself."

"Fighting is not how you earn money or respect."

"There's nothing wrong with being a fighter."

"I didn't say there was; I just don't want my son doing it."

"I'm not going to live my life as 'your son.' I'm going to live it my way. Make my own decisions. Think for myself." Billy bursts out of his room and storms past Jing and me.

Papa comes out, his face red. "I'm sorry you had to hear that," he says to us, then runs down the stairs.

* * *

Neither Papa nor Billy is around for breakfast, but I can't stop hearing their words. Papa never gets mad like that.

The knife sharpener has arrived and is working his grinding wheel out back. Maggy's doing the laundry on the side porch, pouring bluing into the wash water. She scrubs the clothes and feeds them through the wringer. Jing is cleaning the chicken coop. I head out to talk to him.

I haven't said a word about Noah. I hoped Noah would tell Jing how I helped him. Jing must have wondered how Noah got food. Jing had some provisions in his room. Did Noah pretend it was enough? Wouldn't Jing know better?

I want Jing to know I helped Noah. That we're friends. I want it so badly, I think about it all day. "Jing?"

He looks up, scrub brush in hand.

"What's your last name?"

He rolls his tongue into his cheek. "Why?"

"Just wondering."

"In China your last name is your first name. In China, I am Jing Chen. In America, I am Chen Jing."

"What should I call you?"

He peeks out from under his eyebrows. "'Jing' has worked well for us, don't you think?"

"How did you get caught in the quarantine?"

He dunks the scrub brush into the bucket and swishes it around. "I thought I could be helpful, but the situation was already too far gone. I stayed too long, and they wouldn't let me out."

"I'm glad things are back to normal," I say.

"Back to normal." His eyebrows slide up and then down. He takes the wet brush out and begins scrubbing the gate.

"Aren't they?"

He keeps scrubbing. "Thank you for coming for me," he whispers.

I beam. "We tried before. Billy and I. And I tried dressing up like a nurse, but the police stopped me. And then Gus Trotter wrote a letter. Nothing worked."

He stops scrubbing. "I have never dressed as a lady before."

"You looked good."

We laugh.

"I heard you were a leader in Chinatown."

"A leader?" He shakes his head. "I'm just an old magician." He's scrubbing again, his face thoughtful.

"Did you go to college?" I ask.

His eyes grow larger. He stares at me. "Of course not," he mutters.

"You wanted to, though, didn't you?"

His eyebrows furrow. "Why would you say that?"

"You like to read so much. I just . . . wondered."

He nods.

"Did Uncle Karl have something to do with the quarantine?"

"No."

"Are you sure?"

"Yes." He motions with his finger that I should follow him. He pulls three old straw hats off the hooks and puts them onto the tack trunk.

He lifts each hat so I can see there's nothing under it. "Pick one."

I point to the straw hat John Henry took a bite of.

He picks up the hat. Underneath is an egg.

I smile at him. I love this trick. I always have.

"How'd you do it?"

"A magician never tells his secrets."

"You taught Billy."

"Not this one."

"You know a lot that you don't talk about, don't you, Jing?" I whisper.

He picks up the brush and returns to the chicken coop to continue his work. I wait for him to say something else. It's only as I'm walking away that I hear him say: "You're a clever one, Lizzie. I've always known that."

CHAPTER 25

Toil and Toil, Our Maggy Doyle

I take out my pencil to write a poem about Maggy. When I'm done, I read it to her as she cleans the parrot's cage.

Loyal, loyal Maggy Doyle
Does our dishes but has no wishes.
Toil and toil, our Maggy Doyle
Only yearns to water the ferns.

Her face screws up. " 'Yearns'?"

" 'Yearns' means 'wants a lot.' "

She gives me a funny look. "I do not yearn to water the ferns," she mutters.

I laugh. "Well, what do you yearn for?"

She strokes the parrot.

"Maggy?" Nettie calls, stomping through the kitchen door and into the drawing room. She snaps her fingers at Maggy. "I found another one." Maggy closes the parrot in his cage, turns, and follows Nettie.

"Found another what?" I call after them.

"Never you mind, Miss Lizzie. This is between Maggy Doyle and me. Right, Maggy?"

I don't like the sound of this. I follow them to the path on the other side of the Sweeting house, careful not to let them see me.

"There!" Nettie points to the flower bed, bright with nodding daisies.

Maggy leans down, picks up a dead rat, and carries it to the rubbish heap. The Sweetings have five stable boys and five gardeners. There is no reason Maggy should be doing this.

I dash down the path and up the Sweeting stairs. Aunt Hortense has her accounting ledgers fanned out in front of her. "What is it?" she asks.

"Can you come? It's Nettie. She's making Maggy pick up rats."

"Rats?" Aunt Hortense follows me down the steps. Maggy has another dead rat in her hand.

"What is this all about, Nettie?" Aunt Hortense asks.

Nettie's eyes harden when she looks at me. "Nothing to worry about, Mrs. Sweeting. I got it all taken care of, ma'am." Her voice is chipper and sweet.

"Yes, Nettie, I can see that. But I would like to know." Aunt Hortense's eyes drill into Nettie.

"Maggy was just helping us out. That's all. Such a nice woman. Too bad she's . . ." Nettie taps at her head.

"Why are you making her throw out your dead rats?" I ask.

"Nobody wants to touch 'em none," Nettie says. "Maggy, she don't mind."

"Maggy does too mind!" I shout.

Maggy watches me. Aunt Hortense plants her feet. "For goodness' sake, Nettie. You're not to treat Maggy that way."

"But, Mrs. Sweeting, she's asking to do it—"

"She is not!" I stamp my foot.

"Let Maggy speak for herself, Lizzie. Maggy"—Aunt Hortense's voice is gentle—"did you ask Nettie to let you help with this?"

"No, thank you. No, no, no."

"Now, Maggy . . . She don't mean that," Nettie tells Aunt Hortense.

Aunt Hortense arches an eyebrow at Nettie.

"No, no, no." Maggy continues shaking her head.

"Pardon me, ma'am." Nettie grinds her teeth. "I must have been mistaken." We watch her scurry away.

Maggy takes out her polishing cloth and begins work on a garden seat.

"Thank you, Aunt Hortense," I whisper.

"Don't be silly. We can't have our Maggy treated like that."

Aunt Hortense looks at the rats. "The work of Orange Tom, no doubt."

I shake my head. "Orange Tom's gone."

"Gone?" Aunt Hortense frowns. Her eyes shift rapidly right to left. "Must be the new barn cat. Maggy, go with Lizzie and wash your hands. Scrub them like Mr. Kennedy does before surgery."

CHAPTER 26

Pung Yau

The next morning, I find Billy in the corner of the barn, his big hands covered by puffy gloves, punching a burlap bag of potatoes he's hung from the rafters. *Thwack, bunkity, bunkity. Thwack, bunkity, bunkity.* Juliet skitters around in her stall. John Henry hangs in the back. Head up, ears pricked, eyes watchful, not the lazy way he usually stands, resting on one back leg.

Billy slips off his gloves, picks up a rope, and begins jumping. The rope slaps the ground.

"Is Papa still mad?" I ask.

"How should I know," he huffs. His face is red except around his mouth, which is white. Why doesn't that part of his face get red, too?

"What are you doing that makes him so crazy?"

"Thirty-five, thirty-six, thirty-seven," he counts. "Looking out for myself, thirty-eight, thirty-nine."

"Why wouldn't he want that?"

He catches his foot on the rope, stops, and wipes the sweat from his face. "He thinks every conflict should be settled by a bread-and-butter note."

"He does not."

He dribbles water from a bucket into his mouth, and then pours the rest over his head. "People walk all over him."

"No, they don't."

He wipes the water off his face. "Sure they do. Where's Orange Tom, anyway?"

"He's gone."

"And the kittens?" He stares at me.

What do I say to this? "Gone, too," I mumble.

"Is that so?" He puts his gloves back on and whales on the bag again. *Thwack fumba. Thwack.*

When I turn around, Papa is standing behind us in the brown tweed vest and jacket he wears on the road. "Lizzie, I've got a local call. Interested?"

"Of course!"

Papa smiles, his two-dimple smile.

Thwack. Fumba-fumba. Billy hits the potatoes so hard, the bag splits and some of the potatoes spill onto the barn floor.

"Where?" I ask.

"Daisy Bennett's servant girl. How soon can you be ready?"

"Five minutes."

Thwack. Thwack. Fumba. Another potato falls out. Billy's back is to us.

"I need to immunize you both," Papa says.

"From what?" I ask.

"The plague."

"What?" I say.

Billy stops hitting the bag. He turns around.

"It's a precaution . . . that's all. I'd rather not take chances."

"Why do I need to be immunized? I'm not going with you," Billy announces.

"Humor me," Papa says.

"Why should I?" Billy whispers.

Papa's face gets red. "Because I'm your father."

"I don't want to."

Papa takes a breath, sucks in his lips. He turns and walks into the house. I follow him, rolling up the sleeve of my shirtwaist.

In the cold storage room, Papa sets his bag on the table. He unrolls the cloth to reveal a clean syringe. It's Jing's job to boil the syringes and reroll them in clean chamois. Papa takes out a small rectangular bottle marked with an *IP* for the maker. Institut Pasteur. And then it says YERSIN'S ANTI-PLAGUE SERUM. He sticks the needle into the bottle and pulls the stopper back, suctioning the brown serum into the chamber.

" 'Yersin's,' " I say, "rhymes with 'persons.' "

He swabs me with alcohol. The needle pricks. The serum is injected. Papa cleans my arm just as Billy walks in.

I roll down my sleeve. "I read that the plague can look like a bad case of the flu with a terrible headache. Swelling in the groin and black-and-blue marks is how you know."

Billy snorts. "That's what you do in your spare time?"

"Swelling in the lymph nodes, yes," Papa answers me. "But this is just me erring on the side of caution. There's no evidence the plague is here." Papa focuses on Billy. "Change your mind?"

"No," Billy says.

Papa's face falls.

"I'm sorry, Papa," Billy whispers. "It's just, people who get sick get sick. And people who don't, don't. I don't see as how your intervention does much of anything."

"Sometimes it is just a matter of giving comfort, Billy. You're right about that. But immunizations are different. There's real science behind this. They work inside you to stimulate your own immune system to fight the disease. Look, you know how to immunize yourself. I'll leave everything in your room."

Billy doesn't seem to care. But this makes me wonder about Noah. How will he get immunized? And Jing, too, for that matter. It doesn't seem fair that we get immunized but no one else. And what about Gemma and Gus? Papa says this is only a precaution, so I suppose I shouldn't worry.

"Get the picnic basket from Jing. I'll meet you in the barn," Papa tells me.

I run upstairs and change into my softest ribbed stockings and my most comfortable skirt. It may be twenty-four hours before I change my clothes again.

Jing is in the kitchen, wrapping turkey legs for the buggy. My stomach grumbles when I see him.

He nods toward the partially loaded hamper. "Bacon, corn cakes, currant scones."

A happy sigh escapes my lips. Jing smiles.

In the barn, Papa is harnessing Juliet. Jing hands me the food basket, and I place it in its usual spot between the medical bags.

Papa climbs in and gathers the lines, and Juliet prances out.

"Wait." I hear Jing running behind us, my coat with the brown velvet collar in his hands.

The Chinese words for "thank you" float through my head. *"Doh je,"* I say.

Jing stiffens. His eyes register shock. Then a huge smile busts open his face.

"Where'd you learn that?" Papa asks me.

"I found a Chinese-English dictionary," I say.

As we trot onto the street, I run my hand over my arm where it aches from the shot. "You immunized me. Why can't you immunize everyone?"

"Not enough serum. Comes from horses. They lose quite a number before they gather enough for one man."

"The horses die?"

"Sometimes, yes."

"I couldn't stand it if a horse died because of me," I mutter.

"You are more important than any horse, and don't you ever forget it." Papa settles into his seat.

"How did you get the Yersin's?" I ask as we pass a milk wagon driven by a Chinese man with a long braid.

"Medical officers are given immunizations. We have to stay well so we can care for the sick."

"So I'm a medical officer?"

"Today you are." He winks at me. "But this is an accident call. Broken bones, I'm guessing. The girl jumped out of a second-story window."

"Why?"

"Didn't want to be immunized."

Kind of like Billy, I think, though I don't mention this. It would get Papa riled up again.

The dark water of the bay comes in and out of sight as we travel up and down the steep streets. Juliet is breathing hard, her coat shiny with sweat. I rest my head against Papa. He puts his arm around me. He likes it when I go on calls with him.

My father reins Juliet into the Bennetts' small stable. I slip off her harness, then lead her to the watering trough as Papa hurries up to the house.

After giving her a flake of hay from the Bennetts' bale, I climb the steps to the front door. A maid with shocking blue eyes leads me up three stairwells to a tiny dormer room, where a slender Chinese girl in a maid's uniform lies on a narrow cot moaning with pain. Another uniformed Chinese girl, a bit older, stands in the doorway speaking in fast Chinese, the language a barricade.

Papa is in the hall, talking to them in his soothing voice, but the bigger girl has a wild look in her eyes. She won't stop long enough to hear him. I can't understand a word, but her message is clear.

Go away.

"She's in pain. I can help." Papa's voice is gentle.

"You go. Leave alone," the girl says.

The delicate girl in the bed sobs. The other girl stands with her arms crossed. Inside the dormer room are banners of Chinese characters, tasseled baskets full of socks and towels, a bowl of oranges, a pencil sketch of a rooster.

Papa steps closer. "She needs help."

The older girl shouts, then slams the door in his face.

Papa sighs. "Maybe Daisy has someone who can translate." He disappears down the narrow stairwell. The voices continue at a furious pace inside the closed door.

I wish I had the Chinese-English dictionary. I memorized only a few words, and I have no idea how to pronounce them.

"Nei-ho" means "hello." I try this out. *"Nei-ho,"* I say.

Behind the door, the conversation slows. Are they listening?

"Nei-ho," I repeat. And then, *"Pung yao."* Friend.

Now one of the girls is answering me. She's speaking slowly, though I still can't understand.

"Pung yao," I repeat, and then in English, "Open the door. I can help you."

Silence on the other side, then whispers followed by louder rapid-fire Chinese. They seem to be discussing this.

"Pung yao," I whisper, touching my hand to my heart.

The door opens; the girls peer at me.

"I can help," I say. "But only if you let me in."

They nod.

My feet move a step closer. The door remains open. I find a clean cloth in Papa's bag. "Can you get cool water on this?" I ask the bigger girl.

Her eyes fly to my patient. She doesn't want to leave her with me. But the patient nods, and the other girl disappears.

What would Papa do now? "Where does it hurt?" I ask.

"My knee," she answers in English.

"Anywhere else?"

She shakes her head.

"Can I do an examination?"

The girl doesn't respond. I step into the attic room, which smells like oranges. On the shelf is a collection of teacups. An embroidered Chinese dress hangs on a wire. I can only stand up straight in the center of the room.

I perch on the edge of the cot. This girl was so terrified that she jumped out a second-story window. I mustn't scare her again.

Her eyes are glassy with fear, but she's worn down. She knows she needs help.

I examine her as best I can. Scratches are scattered over her neck and face. Her lower arm is badly bruised. She must have landed in a bush. It probably broke her fall.

"Can you move your arms?"

She nods, then shows me. "It's just the knee." She touches her left knee.

"What is your name?"

"Mei," she whispers.

I focus on the knee as Papa comes up the stairs.

"No luck," he calls.

"Mei, this is my papa." I tell her. "He's a doctor. He can help you."

"No!"

I frown. "He can."

"No!" She jerks away and yelps with pain.

"Okay." My hand is up, fingers splayed.

"She's afraid of you, Papa," I call out to him. "Can you tell me what to do?"

My father makes his thinking noise—a popping with his tongue. He rubs his freshly shaved chin. He's too tall for the attic even in the center where the ceiling comes to a point. He stands hunched over, then slides to the floor, settling back on his heels so he can peer into the room as I work. "Okay, Lizzie. . . . We'll take this one step at a time."

"She says her knee hurts."

"Anything else?"

"Minor lacerations."

"Fever?"

"Hard to say. She could be warm from the crying."

"If she has a substantial fever, you'll be able to tell."

I put my hand lightly on her forehead. "No fever."

"Good. That's good. Let's focus on the knee. Left one?"

"Yes."

"Can you help Mei move her leg out of the covers?" I ask Mei's friend, who is hunkered down at the door.

The other girl moves toward the bed and pulls back the quilt, revealing Mei's thin bare leg. The knee looks distorted. No wonder it hurts so much.

Papa looks in. "From here it appears to be a kneecap dislocation," he says. "The question is . . . are there complications? Could be broken bones, sprains."

"How will I know?"

"Ask her how long her knee has been hurting."

"It didn't hurt much at first, but every hour now it gets worse," Mei tells me.

"Did you hear that, Papa?" I ask.

"Yes. Check her ankles, her feet. Go slowly, methodically."

Mei is listening to Papa. She holds her breath as I slowly run my hands along her left leg. When I get to the patella, she winces. "I think it's just the knee."

"Probably the best thing is to give her chloroform and pop it back in. Then see where we are."

"No chloroform!" Mei cries.

"It will help with the pain." Papa's voice is calm.

"No!"

"We'll do it your way, Mei. Lizzie, let me tell you how to slide it back."

Me? Are you crazy? I want to say, but I can't let Mei see I'm afraid, too.

"First, Lizzie, feel your own knee. See in your mind how the patella fits with the tibia and the femur."

"Like the bones in the bone bag," I say.

"Exactly. The impact of the fall popped the kneecap.

Get her friend to hold her, and then gently ease the knee-cap back in place."

Mei's friend's eyes are wary as she stands next to the bed. Mei's face is scrunched up tight. She breathes three big noisy breaths. My hand is trembling. I don't want to hurt her. I glance at my father. He nods encouragingly. And I push the patella back in place. She shrieks. I don't hear the pop, but I feel it.

Tears flow down Mei's cheeks.

"You get it?" Papa calls.

"I think so." That must have hurt like crazy.

"Good. That's good, Lizzie."

"I don't think it's broken."

"No, I don't, either," Papa says.

Mei and her friend are talking in Chinese again. Calm, not angry. Everyone is breathing more easily.

"She can have aspirin," Papa says. "We'll wrap it. Tell her it will be better soon but she needs to stay off her feet as much as possible. No going up and down the stairs. I'll let Daisy know."

Mei nods at me. "I heard. *Doh je, pung yao,*" she whispers to me.

CHAPTER 27

Gus's Idea

"When people get emotional, they can't reason," Papa tells me when we're back in the buggy headed home.

"But jumping out a window rather than getting immunized? That's insanity," I say.

We pass an advertisement for Dr. Blake and his Indestructible Teeth. What could possibly make teeth indestructible?

"Did Mei seem crazy to you?" he asks.

"Not at all."

"I'm guessing no one bothered to give her a proper explanation of why an immunization was required. I wish I'd thought to talk to her about this."

"Were they trying to immunize Mei against smallpox?" I ask.

"The plague."

"The plague? Why would they want to immunize *her*? Mei's not a doctor or the daughter of a doctor."

"Daisy didn't give any details," Papa says as we pass a ragman with his wagon piled high with scraps.

When we get home, my mind churns with questions. Billy refused to get immunized because he knew it would upset Papa. But why would Mei jump out the window?

I start a poem about Mei.

I made a new friend, Mei,
Who jumped from a window today

What rhymes with "patella"? "Fella."

A team clatters across the cobblestone driveway. I peek out the window. The Trotters!

I dash downstairs. In the buggy are Gemma and Hattie.

"Lizzie." Gemma grins. "You have to come. We're sleeping at my house; then we're going to Playland tomorrow. Please say you will. Please." She presses her hands together.

I glance at Hattie. She is still prickly.

"Ask. Then go get your things," Gemma tells me. "We'll help."

Gemma is already out of the buggy, headed into my house, with Hattie behind her. Gemma's faster now that she's off her crutches.

In my room, she sifts through the dresses and shirtwaists in my closet, pushing some to the back, pulling others to the front. She takes out a dress Aunt Hortense bought for me. "How come you never wear this?"

"Too frilly."

"Wear it tomorrow," Gemma commands.

Hattie peeks out the window from behind the blind. "Whose house is that?" She points at the Sweeting mansion.

"Hortense and Karl Sweeting."

She squints at me. "How come you share a driveway with them?"

I don't like the way she asks this. Is she wondering if Papa works for them? "They're my aunt and uncle."

Hattie's mouth drops open. "Karl Sweeting is your uncle?"

I nod, watching her.

"How come you never told anyone?" Hattie demands.

"Why would I tell anyone?"

"You knew, didn't you," Hattie demands of Gemma.

Gemma frowns at her. "What do I care who her uncle is?" She continues instructing me on what I should and shouldn't wear. She tries on my hats, and matches each with a parasol and gloves.

On the way out, I let Jing know I'm visiting the Trotters, and we pile into the coach. I sit between Hattie and Gemma. Hattie can't take her eyes off the Sweeting mansion. Gemma holds my hand while she and Hattie keep up a running chatter about brassieres—a favorite topic.

* * *

When we pull up to the Trotters', Gus is on the porch wearing a black shirt and brown football pants, bouncing a big ball with one hand.

"He's obsessed with that ball," Gemma whispers. "Some new sport, he says."

"Bouncing the ball is a sport?" Hattie asks as she pulls her skirt up just enough so we see her delicate boots and gracefully climbs down out of the carriage.

Gemma shrugs. "Then they run back and forth trying to toss the ball into a fruit basket nailed to the wall. Basketball, he calls it."

"Never heard of it," I say as we walk up to the house.

"Nobody has," Gemma agrees.

In Gemma's room, Gus looks everywhere except directly at me.

Gemma and Hattie hide their giggles behind their hands.

"I need to talk to Lizzie," Gus says.

Hattie doesn't look happy. First Karl and Hortense Sweeting are my uncle and aunt. Now Gus has a message for me.

Gemma's hands fly to her hips. "What's the big secret?"

Gus comes closer and whispers into my ear: "The monkey's dead."

I jump. "Are you sure?"

He nods.

"What did he say? You have to tell us. Did you hear, Hattie?" Gemma asks.

"The monkey's dead," I tell Gemma. "Remember?"

"Does that mean the plague is here?"

"I don't know, Gemma," I say. "I better go home."

Gemma frowns. "Not now. We're going to eat lunch and then spend the night and then go to Playland."

"I can't do that. I have to find out about this," I tell her.

Gemma's hands are on her hips again. "We came all the way over to get you."

"I know. I'm sorry. But I have to talk to Uncle Karl. And Papa's a doctor. He'll come home when he hears about this. He'll need help. So . . . I have to go."

"Don't be crazy. If it's the plague, Lizzie, you can't—"

"I'll drive you," Gus jumps in.

"Whose side are you on?" Gemma demands. Hattie steps closer to Gemma and takes her hand.

"Hers." Gus points to me.

"I'm trying to keep her from getting hurt," Gemma says.

"It's not working," Gus says.

"Thanks a lot," Gemma tells him. "Anyway, you can't drive her without a chaperone." Hattie nods.

"Who's going to know?" Gus crosses his arms.

"I will."

"Gemma!" Gus rolls his eyes at her.

Gemma sighs. "You owe me for this."

"Fine," Gus says.

"I'm sorry," I whisper, then follow Gus out the door.

"Lizzie, wait!" Gemma shouts after me. "Promise me you won't do anything stupid."

I run back to Gemma's room and give her a quick hug. "Don't worry. I'll be fine."

* * *

In the small barn, we climb into the buggy, and the Trotters' stable boy hands the lines to Gus. Gus makes a clicking noise, and the little chestnut trots forward. Out on the street, Gus glances over at me. "That's not all, Lizzie. I heard they were going to burn down Chinatown."

"*What!* Why?"

"I don't know. They hate the Chinese. They want them out."

"You can't just burn down people's houses. That's criminal! They have no right."

"It's not my idea."

"Who? Who is going to do this?"

"I don't know exactly. I don't even know if it's true. I've been asking around because you wanted to know about the monkey." His face turns red.

"When are they going to burn Chinatown?"

"I heard midnight tonight."

"Tonight! Gus, they can't. The police have to stop them!"

"And they will. At least, I think they will."

When we get to the Sweeting mansion, I think Gus will just drop me off. But he hands the horse and carriage to Ho and hurries after me up the marble steps through the thick sweet smell of jasmine. In the foyer, the electric chandelier sparkles. We're already inside by the time the butler appears. I always come in before he has a chance to get the door. He doesn't like this.

I walk Gus through the big kitchen, which smells of banana pudding. Nettie is instructing two houseboys on the correct use of the dumbwaiter. She ignores me. We really don't like each other after what happened with Maggy. I hoped Aunt Hortense would fire her, but she hasn't yet.

Upstairs, Aunt Hortense is on the telephone. I peek into Uncle Karl's office.

Uncle Karl looks pleased to see me. He's wearing a red-striped vest and a white linen suit. A straw boater hangs on the hat rack. "Why, Peanut, you've brought a friend to visit."

"Uncle Karl, this is Gus Trotter."

"Pleased to make your acquaintance, Mr. Trotter," Uncle Karl says.

"You, too, Mr. Sweeting, sir," Gus says.

"We're here because we heard the monkey died," I say, and brace myself.

Uncle Karl groans. "Lizzie! Do you never learn?"

I blunder on. "But, Uncle Karl, if the monkey died, doesn't that mean the plague is here?"

"Poppycock. Hearsay."

"But Dr. Kinyoun injected the plague germ—"

"Kinyoun offed the monkey to prove his point. He had no choice. His reputation was on the line. The quarantine was massively unpopular. He didn't want to look like an ignoramus for having called it."

He pulls the dowels of papers down and begins sifting through them. When he finds the article he's looking for, he sets it in front of me. "Look here." He taps the Chinese words. The translation is handwritten and pasted next to the text. "Even the Chinese can see through these shenanigans."

THE MONKEY IS DEAD

> Why should Chinatown's good name depend on the life and death of a monkey? . . . In the view of this newspaper, the monkey's death was not caused by plague. Alas, the monkey's death was due to starvation—a result of its unlucky encounter with this physician.

I hand the page to Gus to read.

"If this monkey nonsense were true, don't you think I'd splash it all over the front page?" Uncle Karl asks.

"Yes."

"You bet I would. Sell a lot of newspapers, that's for sure."

Uncle Karl will do practically anything to sell more newspapers. I once saw him give free puppies to newsboys who sold more of his newspaper, the *Call,* than of Hearst's *Examiner.*

"Mr. Sweeting, sir." Gus looks directly at Uncle Karl for the first time. "There's talk of burning down Chinatown."

Uncle Karl nods. "I know there is, but it doesn't amount to a hill of beans. Chinatown is in the heart of the city. If they torch it, what's to stop the whole city from burning? It's just talk. Cooler heads will prevail."

"Yes, sir," Gus says.

"Look, I appreciate that you two young people are so civic-minded this afternoon, but on a beautiful day like today . . . I'd head out to Ocean Beach." Uncle Karl stands up to usher us out. "Shall I arrange a ride for you?"

"Not right now. Thanks, Uncle Karl," I say.

Uncle Karl has made me feel better. Burning down Chinatown. Who would do that? Still, something he said niggles. He said a fire in Chinatown would put the city at risk. It's as if he's not worried about Chinatown, only the rest of the city.

Gus and I walk down the formal stairwell. I always use the servants' stairs, but if I take Gus that way, it will make Aunt Hortense crazy.

Outside on the cobblestones between the houses, Gus points to a dead rat. "We've had way more dead rats than usual this year, have you noticed?"

"Yes, and our mouser has run away. Seems we should have fewer dead ones lying around."

"At school we've been reading about London in Shakespeare's time. They had the plague then. They think Shakespeare's sisters died of it."

"Really?" Gus is so smart.

"Yep . . . and they talk about all the rats."

"Papa says rats are connected to lots of diseases."

Gus nods. "I suppose, but that's not the only thing that bothers me. When people try so hard to prove something isn't true, it makes me suspicious."

"So what are you saying, Gus? You think the plague is here?"

"I wonder."

"Well, Papa says there are no confirmed cases," I tell him.

Gus climbs into his buggy. "Then I'm wrong. He'd know."

"Gus?"

"Yes." He turns back to me. "Thank you for finding out and for bringing me home. You're a good"—my face gets hot—"you know, friend."

"Oh, um, yes." He turns away, but not before I see the brilliant smile flash across his lips.

After dinner, I spot Billy in the stable saddling John Henry.

I run to the barn in my stocking feet. "Where are you going?"

"Nowhere."

"Do you know when Papa will be back?"

"I think Jack Clemons took him up to San Rafael. His wife had a seizure. Be at least a day before we'll see him again."

"Can I ask you something?"

"Shoot."

"Gus was talking about people burning down Chinatown. Have you heard anything about that?"

Billy's eyes shift slightly. He slips the bit into John Henry's mouth. "Why?"

"Why? Because it's important."

"Is Jing here?"

"No."

"Where is he?"

"I don't know."

"When's he coming back?" Billy pulls the reins over John Henry's ears and then flaps them over the pommel.

"I don't know that, either," I say. "Hey, wait. You know something."

"No." His voice falters.

"You do."

Billy places the toe of his boot in the stirrup. "I don't know anything!"

"Billy." I hang on his arm like I used to when we were little and I wanted something. "Tell me."

"Stop being annoying. Look." He shakes me off, turns, and looks straight into my eyes for once. I see the old Billy then. He's there behind the new one. "I'm in a fight tonight. Got a big purse. I don't want to be worried about you. Stay out of this, all right?"

"*You* worry about *me*?"

"It happens," he snorts. I let go of him, and he gets onto John Henry.

"Shakespeare's sisters died of the plague," I tell him.

"Bully for Shakespeare's sisters. You're not going to die of the plague. But you might stick your nose where it doesn't belong."

"Uncle Karl said they aren't going to burn Chinatown down."

"He's right, so go inside, Lizzie, like a good girl." He whacks John Henry with his crop and the big horse trots forward.

"Can't I come with you?"

"No. Go in the house or I'll tell Aunt Hortense. I mean it!"

The Night Ride

I'll stay out of it once I've let Noah and Jing know to get out of Chinatown. I hope Uncle Karl is right, but there's no way I'm going to sit around the house. I need to warn them, even if it means lying to Aunt Hortense again. Billy would only say stay away if there were something going on.

Navigating Chinatown's narrow streets with a horse and buggy is too hard. Billy could barely manage. And if I took the wagon, who would watch it while I searched for Noah?

I could put on my overalls and ride Juliet bareback, but Aunt Hortense would kill me. She'd rather I rode in my birthday suit. She doesn't even approve of split skirts. If I ride past her window, she'll hear me.

My only hope is to go after she falls asleep. This time I

won't be so stupid as to use Uncle Karl's name. She doesn't know about Noah. She won't find out about this, either. I'll be back before she wakes up.

As I wait in my overalls, the big yellow moon high in the night sky, my hands shake and my knees wobble. Maggy is asleep. Jing isn't back yet.

The Sweeting bedroom is on the other side of their mansion, but what about the servants? The Irish sleep on the fourth floor, and the Chinese sleep in the basement. Will they hear? Two hunting dogs are kept in the stable at the far corner of their property. Will Aunt Hortense and Uncle Karl assume their dogs are barking at a skunk? Or send someone to investigate?

I tie my hair back, take Billy's old cap off the hat rack, and let myself out the back door. The sounds of the door shutting, my steps on the footpath, even my breathing, seem unnaturally loud. Someone is going to hear.

In our barn, Juliet is lying down in her straw bed. My presence startles her, and she gets up. She knows I shouldn't be here at this hour.

The windowless tack room is pitch-black. Light a gas lamp? No. If a maid or a stable boy looks out, they'll see a light and know something is amiss. I feel my way through the bridles to what I think is Juliet's, but when I get it out to the moonlight, I see it's an old one with a busted throat-latch.

Back I go, running my hands along each bit, until I find another round snaffle ring. This time I'm right.

In my overalls I've packed money, matches, and a cookie.

I'd like to ride with a light, but I can't gallop holding a lantern. There's a full moon out tonight. Juliet should be fine.

I stick my finger into the flat space behind Juliet's teeth; she opens her mouth for the bit, and I slip the headstall over her ears. Then I lead her to the mounting block, lace my hands through her dark mane, get a firm hold of the reins, and slide my leg over her warm back.

One horse is quieter than a horse and a buggy or a horse and a wagon, but hooves on the cobblestones make a racket. My plan is to ride on our grass until the last possible moment, then cut across to the cobblestones for the final ten feet.

Juliet knows me well. I don't have to kick her to get her to move. A slight squeeze will do. Sometimes I just think what I want and she does it.

I huddle over Juliet's mane as we trot along the grass. My heart pumps with the thrill of riding in the crisp night air. I steer her around the last tree and onto the driveway. Her hooves clatter as we trot through the gate. But when I turn back to look, nothing stirs.

The street is dark and quiet. A lamplighter tends to a gaslight; electric porch lights flicker. The wind cuts through my jacket; the night is colder than I expected.

In the distance I hear a horse snort, a drunken man's song, the clanking of metal.

I keep Juliet trotting down the center of the street, away from the dark alleys. Aunt Hortense's voice runs through my head. *This is no place for a young lady, Elizabeth.* For once, she's right. If I were to disappear right now, it would be morning before anyone knew, and that might be too late.

The girls from Miss Barstow's talk about people getting "shanghaied." Out of the darkness, someone grabs you and hits you over the head. When you wake up, you're on a ship sailing for Shanghai or some other place halfway around the world. Some eventually make it home. Most do not.

The road is flat on this block. I urge Juliet to gallop before the steep hills begin again and I have to pull her back to a jog. I pass a few buggies and men on foot coming home from the saloons, but no one pays any attention to me. In the dark, with my short hair, Billy's cap, and my overalls, I look like a boy.

Up and down the streets we go. When the street is level again, I squeeze Juliet's warm sides, and she breaks into a gallop. She's breathing hard.

Up ahead, an abandoned wagon blocks the road. I pull her up. Juliet prances, roots with her head. I wheel her back around the way I came, but when I turn, five men appear out of the darkness.

In front of me, the men. Behind me, the wagon.

"Purty horse," a young man with a scruffy beard says.

They form a wall in front of me. Juliet senses my terror and spins. The short one with sweaty, shiny skin has brass knuckles.

I consider the wagon. It's too big to jump. Could we squeeze through? No.

"Why, she's a girl, ain't she?' says the tall one who is missing most of his teeth. He has a raspy laugh.

"A horse and a girl. Looks like we hit the jackpot."

"You give us that horse, little girl, and maybe we'll let you go," Scruffy Beard says.

"Or maybe we won't." The short one smells of rum and urine.

A man with a bull chest has a knife. I see it glint.

They're closing in. I leap off, slip my fingers under the headstall, and pull Juliet's bridle off. I swing the bridle hard and hit Juliet on the butt with the bit; she bolts through the men. With no bridle on and no saddle, she's impossible to catch. In the commotion, as they chase her, I run for my life.

My feet fly over the street, footsteps right behind me. I pick up speed, glancing back. There's more room between us now, but just as I turn around, my foot twists and I fly through the air and slam hard into the street. Scruffy Beard leaps onto me before I can get up. I don't see his face. But I can feel his beard. Smell his sweat.

I yank free, but a cold arm like a metal pipe wraps around my chest. A second arm has me by the throat.

I scream. The arm tightens, cutting off the sound. Bull Chest knocks the back of my knees with a metal bar, and my legs cave. I collapse forward, his chest bearing down on me. I gasp in the smell of his rotting teeth, try to kick out. Try to shove him off.

Think, think, I tell myself, but my mind has gone dark. That's when Billy's voice comes to me. *There are points on a person, Lizzie, that will kill them. Temple, armpit, liver, groin. Behind the ear.*

With a sudden shock of power, I bust my arm out of Bull Chest's lock and hit him as hard as I can behind his ear. He yelps and loosens his grasp for one second, and I pull free. Scruffy Beard catches my leg. I yank it loose; the denim rips. I run like fire.

Honolulu

My heart beats fast. My teeth chatter. I run past Chinatown, trying to figure out where to stop. The Chinatown streets are lively even this late. So different from how it was during the quarantine. A gambling parlor is lit up with gaslight. One of the shops is open, its window crammed with dried sea horses, snakes, birds, crabs, live ducks, and green frogs. I keep running, terrified that the men are still following, though when I look back—no one. I'm dripping sweat, but the wind chills me. I just want to go home, but I have to warn Noah.

I remember once he told me he lives in an alley off Kearny, but I have no idea where that is. All the street signs are in Chinese.

My cap is gone. My hair has fallen down around my shoulders. No mistaking me for a boy now.

I check my locket watch. Eleven-thirty. I only have a half hour! I need to ask someone for help. But who?

I hope for a white man. But I feel more comfortable asking someone like Jing. I trust him more than anyone else, even Uncle Karl. A wave of guilt comes over me. What a thought!

Still, it couldn't be a white man, because a white man won't be able to read the street signs. How many white men know Chinese?

An old man with a short beard walks by. But he has a sour face. I can't bring myself to ask him. A younger man watches from across the street. The way he looks at me makes me shudder.

I pass by three other men, but none seem right. Where are the women?

Then I spot a kid, maybe nine years old. He has a stick in his hand, and he's running it along an iron railing. *Rappity fump. Rappity fump.* What's he doing out so late?

"Hey? Can I ask you something?"

The boy turns. His eyes are watchful, but he doesn't run away.

"Look," I say, "do you know a boy named Noah?"

He whacks his stick against his pantaloons. He doesn't answer, but I can tell he knows.

"Could you take me to him?" I lower my voice. "I'm a friend of Six of Six."

A shock of surprise registers in his eyes. "Six of Six . . . *you?*"

"Yes."

The boy frowns. "You look like a girl."

I shrug.

"No girl could be a friend of Six of Six."

"How would I know about it otherwise?"

He peers at me. "What's Noah's Chinese name?"

"Choy."

The boy nods reluctantly. "Could go get him . . . maybe," he mutters.

He's afraid to show a strange white girl where Noah lives. But we don't have time, and I can't stand out here by myself. What if those men come for me?

"I want to go with you."

He shakes his head. I reach into my pocket and pull out a nickel.

The boy inspects the nickel in the moonlight. He tests the weight in his palm, then slips it into his pocket. I follow him down a shadowy alley, which gets darker and darker. I put my hand out, feeling my way. The wall is grimy. I can barely see the boy. Where is he leading me?

My panic rises as the dark presses in. In front of me a door squeaks, opening to a barely visible space. I grab the boy's shirt. I can hardly breathe.

And then—smoke. The smell is thick in my nostrils. Have they started? Are they burning Chinatown? Why did I come here? *I'll be burned alive.*

But no. Cigarettes. Only cigarettes. Tiny red circles of fire in the night. We're walking by people smoking cigarettes. I let go of the boy's shirt.

We go left, down rickety metal stairs that creak from

our weight. The banister sways, and I yank my hand back. The sound echoes in the stairwell.

At the bottom, my feet hit hard dirt. I follow the boy behind a paper screen and through another doorway.

Behind me footsteps. My heart thumps. I grab his shirt again. "Someone's coming," I whisper.

"It's next door."

We walk across an underground room, this one darker than the last. Something smells awful. I hold my breath for as long as I can, then gasp. My stomach clenches; food shoots up my throat. I barely manage to keep it down. A sick taste in my mouth.

"What is that smell?" I whisper.

"Never mind."

That's when I remember the matches in my pocket. I strike one. In a flash I see the tiny, cluttered room. Tables and chairs are shoved on top of each other, and barrels are piled high. Each barrel is closed, except one has shoes.

It's not just shoes.

It's feet.

A cry comes out of my throat before I can stop it.

A body is rolled in the barrel. Another is stuffed into a burlap sack, just the knees visible. The match goes out.

"They're dead," I whisper, striking another match.

The boy doesn't answer. My skin crawls. My mouth goes dry. "Are you sure this is the way to Noah?"

"Yes. The safe way."

This is the safe way? I try to light another match, but my hand is shaking too hard. I keep walking.

"I'm not supposed to be out. My father might see me if I take you the other way."

I follow even closer. *Don't leave me here.*

We're walking up two sets of stairs to a courtyard. The boy heads for a skinny door—half the width of a normal one, two thirds the height. He knocks.

No one answers.

He knocks again. *Please let this be Noah.*

The door cracks open. I nearly wet my pants. And then Noah!

His eyes are wide. "Lizzie, what!"

I hug him. I don't want to let him go. The boy watches, his eyes flickering with fascination. Noah talks to him in Chinese. The boy answers back, his tone full of questions. Noah shakes his head, his voice definite. The boy disappears.

"Noah, I heard they're coming. They're going to burn down Chinatown. Tonight at midnight. We have to get out of here. You and Jing need to come home."

Noah gasps. He closes his eyes, and when he opens them, he's breathing hard as if he's been running. He shakes his head. "I deserted them for the quarantine. I can't do that again."

"But what's the sense of staying and getting hurt?"

"You warned me. Now go home, Lizzie. It isn't safe here." I follow him into a small room. There's a barrel of rice with an abalone shell dipper, neat stacks of newspapers against one wall, and a rack of bright silk clothes against another.

"If you don't go, I won't, either," I say, though I sound braver than I feel. Part of me wants to help Noah. The other part doesn't want to go back home alone.

"Is Jing here?" I pray he is. He'll keep me safe. He always has. *Please let him be here.*

"He's on his way back to your house," Noah tells me as a furry orange tail thrashes out from behind a bolt of cloth.

"Orange Tom!"

Noah nods. "I tried to get him to go back. He wouldn't."

"He likes you."

"Yes . . ." He takes my hand. "We've got to go."

"Where is your uncle Han?"

"At a meeting of the Six Companies."

We take a different way back up to the mouth of Chinatown. Noah stops and knocks on doors as we go. He warns them in fast Chinese, his hands gesturing wildly. "Honolulu" is the only word I recognize. Soon boys are scurrying after us.

"Noah," I whisper, "why were there dead bodies in those barrels? That kid took me past them on the way to you."

Noah does a double take. "Shhh," he whispers. "We aren't allowed to talk about that."

The boys following us are mostly Noah's age. Six of Six, I'm guessing, though there are more than six.

Word spreads through the streets. "Honolulu! Honolulu!" they all cry.

"What does that mean?" I ask.

"They burned down Chinatown in Honolulu when

there was a plague outbreak. Everybody was afraid this would happen here."

We're running now. There seems to be a plan. They were expecting this.

"Honolulu! Honolulu!"

Some hold paper lanterns, kerosene lamps, candles. Boys are dressed in bright Chinese pants and blouses. They are in short pants and dark jackets. Others are all in black.

In the distance we hear the sound of horses. The shouts of men. We see the flash of torches. There are hoots and hollers in the dark night, some twenty men on horseback and on foot.

Are the men who attacked me out there? I grab Noah's hand. Noah wraps his fingers around mine. He won't let go.

"Noah!" I shout, but he can't hear me over the roar of the approaching mob. My arms tremble. My hands shake. I squeeze Noah's hand as Papa's words float through my head. *Courage comes from your heart, not your fists.*

Noah stands in the road. One boy, his hand raised. My throat feels frozen. I stand next to him, my hand in his. Together we raise our linked hands. Soon the others fall in . . . a line of silent boys, hands raised in the night.

The first of the mob sees us. Their torches are held high, burning bright.

"Get out of the way!" someone shouts. Some horses have stopped; others keep trotting toward us. There are men on foot. There are men with knives.

We are just a bunch of kids standing together in one wobbly line.

We can't fight them. We're outnumbered. We have to outthink them.

More men join the mob.

My heart beats loudly in my head.

"Hey, hey, excuse me. Move out of the way." A brown horse gallops toward us. Juliet!

I gasp. Those men caught her! They've come to get me.

But the tall rider is Billy. Billy has Juliet!

"Lizzie, what are you doing? Get out of there! Didn't I tell you to stay home?" Billy shouts.

"Get her out of here!" a big man in fisherman's thigh-high boots shouts. Others join him.

But I'm not leaving Noah. "Billy, help us!" I shout.

Juliet is walking across the space between the Chinese and the mob. "Come on, Lizzie," Billy says in the voice he uses to gentle a horse.

I don't move.

"Get her out of here. We're going to torch this place."

"They're stealing our jobs."

"Send 'em back to China."

"Burn it! Burn it!" they shout.

My mind freezes. We can't stop them. I look at the glistening torches. And then suddenly in a rush it all makes sense. The monkey's death, the feet in barrels.

Papa and Uncle Karl are wrong. The plague is here. But everyone is hiding it. Is there a way to use that now?

"It's the plague," I shout. "The monkey died. We know for sure. If you catch it, there'll be nobody to protect the city."

"That ain't true," someone yells.

"All the more reason to let it burn," another man shouts. "Keep it from spreading."

"Burn it out!" they shout.

"Why you in there? Aren't you afraid you'll get sick?" somebody else shouts.

"If the plague's here, burn it out!" a voice bellows from back in the crowd.

"Burn it! Burn it!" Others take up the cry.

"Lizzie!" Billy again.

"You can't burn it." My voice is strong. "Ask the rich people. Ask them if the monkey died. Ask them what that means. You go in there, *you'll* catch the plague. They won't."

"Don't make no sense," someone else says. "Why'd you go in there if the plague is there?"

"I've been immunized," I say.

"Immu-what?" someone asks.

"It's medicine. A shot so I don't get the plague."

"That true?"

"Yes!" I shout.

"Can I get me one?" someone else calls.

"How 'bout me?"

"Me! Me!" The voices call from all around.

The mob is breaking apart. Some want to be immunized. Others just want to see Chinatown burn. The men in the back hoot for burning, but some turn back.

“The monkey’s dead. It means any of us could die. Don’t go in there,” I shout.

“The monkey’s dead. The monkey’s dead.” We all pick up the call.

“Anybody can die. Go in there, you’ll be next!” Billy’s voice booms over the rest.

The small group in the back is moving forward, fire in their eyes. The leader on the small gray horse turns on them. “You immu-nozed? Any of you? You want to die?”

“Ain’t going to die. Just burn the place. That’ll take care of it.”

“The plague. You numskulls ever heard of it? Deadliest disease in the world.”

The Chinese are on one side with me. The mob on the other. Billy and Juliet stand between us.

“He’s right!” Billy says. “You catch it, you die.”

“Hey, ain’t that the fighter we saw the other night?”

“Billy!” somebody shouts. “It’s Billy!”

Billy waves to them. “I’m the doctor’s son. I know. It’s dangerous to go in there. Don’t risk it.”

“Got to get rid of it. How we going to do that?” somebody else shouts.

“Go on, then,” the mob leader shouts. “You want to kill yourself . . . it ain’t a pretty way to go.”

“Burn it down. We can’t catch nothing.”

“It don’t work like that!”

“Best thing is to go home.” I hear a familiar voice. Out of the darkness, Gus appears! He trots his gray mare to our side. Gus stands with us.

"The rats!" Gus shouts. "Kill the rats! They spread the disease. That will get rid of it."

This is such a smart thing to say. True or not, it gives the mob something to do.

"Kill the rats!" Billy takes up the cry.

"Kill the rats!" we all shout. "The rats! The rats! The rats!"

CHAPTER 30

The Servants Vanish

On the way home, I ride double behind Gus. Where exactly do I put my hands? How do I keep my legs from touching his? What if Aunt Hortense sees this? If there's anything more improper than riding bareback on your own, it's riding bareback behind a boy.

"How'd you know I'd be there?" I ask him.

"I'm starting to see how you operate."

It seems after what I've been through, the least of my worries should be riding behind Gus, but it's practically all I think about the whole ride home. Being a girl is complicated. But it isn't all bad, I have to admit.

Noah rides behind Billy. Billy seems to know that Noah is Jing's son. How?

Gus lets me off in front of the gate. The fewer horses

that clatter across the driveway, the better. Nobody wants to wake Aunt Hortense. Noah slips wordlessly up the back stairs. Billy and I put Juliet away.

"Did you win?" I ask Billy, rubbing Juliet's legs with liniment.

He shakes his head. "Nope."

"I'm sorry."

"That's okay. I have another plan."

"For how to make the money?"

"Yep."

"At least you don't look like you got beat up too badly this time. How'd you know I'd be there, anyway?" I ask, checking Juliet's water trough.

"I came home and put John Henry away. I was just finishing when Juliet trotted up, no bridle, no saddle. I ran upstairs to see if you were there. When you weren't, it wasn't hard to figure out where you'd be. You are such an idiot. Don't you realize how dangerous that was?"

"How'd you know about Noah?"

He smiles his most charming Billy smile as he tosses a flake of hay into Juliet's manger. "I went up to see the kittens."

"You met him?"

"I found the poem you wrote for him."

"But you didn't tell anyone."

"Do I look like a squealer? Look." He stops, brushing the hay out of his hair. "Keep this quiet, okay? There's more to Aunt Hortense than you think. But she'll never in a million years understand this."

"I know," I say, closing Juliet's stall door.

* * *

Upstairs, I head for Maggy's room like I used to right after Mama died. Maggy sits up in bed. "Miss Lizzie?"

I curl up in her bed. She strokes my hair as I tell her everything that happened. It doesn't matter if she doesn't understand it all. What matters is that she's here and she accepts me just as I am. When I'm finished telling her the whole long story, she settles me into my own bed.

In the kitchen the next morning, Jing is there, serving hotcakes. Our eyes watch each other. It's only the two of us. But he knows I know, and that makes all the difference.

"Why didn't you tell us about Noah?"

He nods as if he's been expecting this question. He wipes his hands on a dish towel. "It wouldn't have been fair."

"Fair?" I frown at him.

"Mr. and Mrs. Sweeting would not have liked it. If I had told you, it would have put you and your papa in an awkward position. Against your own flesh and blood. It was my secret; it seemed unfair to burden you with it."

As much as I hate to admit it, he's right.

"I'm glad I got to meet him. Is he still here?"

"Not for long."

I nod. "Jing? Somebody's hiding the bodies of people who died of the plague in Chinatown, aren't they?"

He eyes me carefully. "It isn't just Chinatown. They're hiding them everywhere. Shipping them out on carts, on train cars, in cargo holds. Doctors are falsifying death certificates. Nobody wants to believe what's happening."

"Why?"

"Some are terrified. Others think it's bad for business. There's all kinds of finger-pointing and misinformation."

"We have to get everyone immunized," I say. "It's the only solution."

"No!" His face is red; his nostrils flare.

"It's science, Jing. It's like the electric lights. Remember how we didn't believe that would work, either?"

He shakes his head, his face stony.

Half of my father's patients think evil spirits cause disease. They're certain a charm hung on a ribbon, a rabbit's foot, or an astrology chart is more effective than real medicine. But this is Jing. He's not like that.

I stand in front of him. "I was immunized. I can't get the plague."

Jing turns and walks out the door.

In the parlor, the dark night cloth still hangs over the parrot, Mr. P. "Maggy Doyle," the parrot chirps. "Maggy Doyle. Maggy Doyle."

Strange, I've never heard the parrot say that before. Pretty much all he says is "dirty work" and "supper's ready."

My boots are in Maggy's room. I go back up to get them. The hall is silent. Her door is closed. "Maggy? Are you up here?"

I knock. "Maggy?"

No answer.

I crack open the door. The room is hot and stuffy. Maggy is on her bed, shiny with sweat.

"Maggy!" I touch her forehead; heat radiates through my hand.

"You're sick," I whisper.

She moans. Her eyes are closed, and her arms are crossed in front of her.

I try to think clearly as if this were a patient and not Maggy. Papa would wash his hands. He would take time to gather the supplies he needs. He would bring cool cloths for her fever, then examine her. He wouldn't jump to conclusions. He would remain calm.

I go downstairs, wash up, and get what I need.

Back in Maggy's room, I take the towel from her dresser, pour water into the bowl and soak the towel. Then I lay the cool cloth on her forehead, loosen her apron and high-collared shirtwaist. She must have gotten dressed for work but was too sick to leave her room.

I give her a sponge bath, gentle with her the way she is with me. I try to get her to take a sip of water.

Examining Maggy feels strange. But who is there to take care of her? Papa is gone. Dr. Roumalade won't treat a servant. There is only me. I need to find out as much as I can so I know how to help her.

"Maggy." I try to make my voice as soothing as Papa's. "I'm going to take care of you."

"No." She sits up straight in bed.

"It's okay," I whisper.

"Maggy works for Miss Lizzie," Maggy says, trying to get out of bed.

"Today is opposite day," I say. "Lizzie is going to work for Maggy."

"Opposite day?"

Her arms relax, and she sinks back into bed. Then she begins shaking, thrashing, kicking off her covers.

I take a deep breath and examine her.

It's when I get to her left armpit that my hand begins to tremble. In the soft tissue of her lymph nodes are bruised swellings.

A drip of sweat slips down my back.

Don't jump to conclusions, Papa's voice in my head reminds me. It could be a bruise. Carefully I check the right armpit, where I see the same thing a bit fainter and not in the same spot.

Maggy's eyes are closed, her head sunk back into the pillow. She's half-asleep, mumbling, talking like she sometimes does when she works. I get the worn old stuffed bear she keeps on her dresser and place it next to her.

"I'll be back." I dash down the stairs just as Jing is coming up. "Maggy's sick," I tell him.

His eyebrows rise.

"It looks like the plague," I mumble.

I see the shock in his eyes, then run to Billy's room. Billy is still asleep. I gently wake him. "Billy, we need Papa. You have to get him *now*!"

"What?"

"You said Papa was in San Rafael. You said you knew where. Can you find him? It's Maggy . . . I think, I'm afraid . . . it's the plague."

Billy's sits straight up in bed. "Get out of here so I can get dressed."

A minute later he bolts out of the room, leaps down the stairs, grabs a cinnamon roll, heads to the barn, hooks the wagon to John Henry, and is gone.

I head for the cold box in the cold storage room, where Papa keeps his medicine. The bottles are in alphabetical order. Acetanilide, arnica, belladonna, bichloride of mercury . . . paregoric. No bottles say "Yersin's."

I search the cabinets—bandages, scalpels, magnifying glasses, ointments, brace. Not a single bottle of Yersin's Plague Antiserum. I don't even know if it will work, now that she has it, but it's the only thing I can think to do.

Papa has a small practice. Maybe they didn't give him much. But what about Billy's dose? If I can find it, should I give it to Maggy? I wish I'd asked Billy before he left.

Did he immunize himself with the Yersin's? It's only one vial, and everybody needs it. Jing, Noah, Aunt Hortense, Uncle Karl, Maggy, Gemma, Gus, and Hattie. And all of those men last night. Papa said there isn't enough Yersin's.

How can you decide one life is more valuable than another?

I try to calculate how long it will take Billy to get to San Rafael and then for Papa and Billy to get home. One day. Is that too long for Maggy?

No one survives the hospital. It's unthinkable to send

anyone there. We need Dr. Roumalade, but how do we get him here for a servant?

Aunt Hortense likes Maggy. Can she persuade Roumalade to treat her?

I dash down the stairs and across the way to the Sweeting kitchen, where the quiet stuns me. No clanging of pots and rolling pins. Where is everyone? What happened?

"Aunt Hortense!" I panic, running through the empty rooms. The house echoes. "Aunt Hortense! Please!"

"Aunt Hortense!" I run up the grand stairwell and down the servants' stairs. I check the Irish quarters, then go down to the Chinese floor and back into the kitchen and dining room. Up the stairs to the music room. The whole house, as big as a hotel, is deserted.

What if Aunt Hortense is sick? She always worries about me, but I never think about her. It's just like Mama. I paid no attention, and then she was gone.

I hurry outside to the Sweeting stable. The horses are there. "Aunt Hortense!" I shout. "Don't leave me, too." The tears run down my cheeks.

"Aunt Hortense!" I run up to our stable, my feet pounding the walkway.

And then she's here. Slipping and sliding in her fashionable boots, wearing a lavender dress that hangs loosely without her corset. Her hair is down. No hat or gloves. She reminds me so much of Mama this way.

"Lizzie," she cries.

"I love you, Aunt Hortense. Do you love me?" My voice is cracking. The feelings are rising up in my chest, clogging my throat. She wraps her arms around me.

"Of course I love you, Lizzie. You and Billy are more important to me than anything else in the world. Don't you know that? Did you think I'd put up with all your nonsense if I didn't love you so much?"

"Maggy's sick. I think it's the plague. I read up on it. Fever, small bruised marks, a swelling in her armpit."

Aunt Hortense freezes. The shock hits her hard.

"Are you sure?"

"Pretty sure."

"Where is she?"

"Her room. Aunt Hortense." My throat is thick with fear. I can hardly get the words through it. "What about you? Have you been immunized?"

She nods. "Dr. Roumalade immunized me. Yersin's. Cost a pretty penny, too. Your papa told me he immunized you."

I let out my breath. For a minute I just hold her, my arms trembling, aching with gratitude that she looked after herself.

"Can you call Dr. Roumalade? Will he come for Maggy?"

Aunt Hortense frowns, considering this. "Mr. Sweeting will get Roumalade."

"He won't treat her."

"He will if Mr. Sweeting insists."

"Will Uncle Karl do that?"

Aunt Hortense looks at me. "I'll make certain he does."

Whatever Uncle Karl's faults, he can bring Roumalade out when we need him. No one else could do that.

Rhymes with "Persons"

"Mr. Sweeting! Mr. Sweeting!" Aunt Hortense shouts, half-running after Uncle Karl's motorcar.

Uncle Karl stamps on the brakes. The motorcar sputters and dies. "What's the matter?"

"Lizzie thinks Maggy has the plague." Aunt Hortense's hands are holding each other so tightly, her fingertips are red.

"Not possible. Where is your father, Peanut?"

"San Rafael," Aunt Hortense answers for me.

"Billy has gone for him," I say.

"Can you get Dr. Roumalade?" Aunt Hortense asks.

"Calm yourself, Mrs. Sweeting!" Karl tells her as he climbs out of the horseless carriage.

"Will you get him?" she shouts.

"Of course I will. But it's not the plague. You're getting yourself worked up for nothing."

"Elizabeth thinks it is."

"With all due respect, Mrs. Sweeting, our Peanut is a thirteen-year-old girl. This is Roumalade's province. Not ours," Uncle Karl barks.

Aunt Hortense nods, but when his back is turned, she whispers into my ear, "See if you can find any more Yersin's, Lizzie. Go now!"

I run to the cold storage room again. It has to be here. I must have missed it before. I tear the place apart looking for a bottle marked with *IP* for "Institut Pasteur."

When I return, Dr. Roumalade is making his way out of the Sweetings' motorcar.

Dr. Roumalade straightens his coat. He reaches into the back for his doctor's bag. Aunt Hortense pounces on him. "It's our Maggy Doyle. . . . There's talk of the plague."

"The plague? And how has this been determined?" Dr. Roumalade takes off his hat and smoothes his bald head.

"My niece examined her. Jules Kennedy's daughter." Aunt Hortense nods toward me.

Dr. Roumalade snorts. "A girl has diagnosed the plague? Forgive me, Mrs. Sweeting, but—"

"I told you it was nonsense," Uncle Karl tells Aunt Hortense.

Believe in yourself. Papa's voice in my head reassures me. "I know what I saw."

"You're going to take a child's word for it, when every doctor worth his salt knows these plague rumors are untrue?" Uncle Karl says. "The president of Cooper Medical College has assured us there is no plague, woman!"

Dr. Roumalade turns to me. "Does your father believe the plague is here?"

I shake my head miserably.

"Her own father doesn't agree with her. Why are we taking a child's silly ideas so seriously," Dr. Roumalade asks Aunt Hortense.

I take a step back, ready for Aunt Hortense to tell me I'm wrong.

"Lizzie." Aunt Hortense's voice is low and strong. "What are the signs of the plague?"

"Hard red lumps in her groin and armpits, fever, black-and-blue marks, headache, dizziness, nausea."

"She read up on it. Does that make her an expert?" Dr. Roumalade asks.

"Maggy has all of them?" my aunt asks. Her attention is on me.

"Yes, ma'am."

Karl looks to Dr. Roumalade. "Surely there are half a dozen illnesses that present this way."

"Not with lumps in the armpits and black-and-blue marks." My voice comes out boldly. I know what I saw.

Roumalade clears his throat. "I'll need to examine her."

"Of course," Aunt Hortense says. "But, Doctor, why would you immunize us if you knew the plague wasn't here?"

Dr. Roumalade's lips shift. "No harm in being cautious."

Uncle Karl takes a bite of his cigar. He watches Dr. Roumalade make his way to our house. "I can't live it down if Hearst is right. You know that, don't you?" he tells Aunt Hortense.

"For the love of God, Mr. Sweeting, I don't care if Hearst is right."

All I can do is pray that when Dr. Roumalade examines Maggy, he'll know how to help her. He's the doctor for the railroad and Comstock millionaires. They wouldn't hire a second-rate physician, would they?

I pace back and forth outside Maggy's room. We need Papa. Has Billy found him? Should we send everyone away, or keep them inside? And what about the yellow plague flag? . . . Should we hang it?

When Roumalade finally finishes, he walks right by me without a word. I chase after him down our two flights of stairs and across the way to the Sweeting house. "Dr. Roumalade? Dr. Roumalade?"

He ignores me.

In the Sweetings' kitchen, he confers with Uncle Karl.

The kitchen is silent except for their hushed whispers. Aunt Hortense and I stand in front of the stove, waiting to hear.

"Where are all the servants?" I ask.

"Gone," Aunt Hortense says.

"Gone?"

"Last night, they heard 'the plague,' and they took off."

I think about the mob in Chinatown. Everybody is afraid.

"I tried to explain about immunization, but I couldn't make myself understood. The more I said, the more upset they got," Aunt Hortense says.

"It's the same way with the smallpox vaccine. People have a hard time believing it will help."

"It's not just that. There was some kind of crazy article in Hearst's paper. A reporter got immunized with Haffkine's, and then he wrote about the side effects. Scared them all half to death," Aunt Hortense says.

Dr. Roumalade and Uncle Karl have finished. Uncle Karl beckons for Aunt Hortense.

I can hardly wait to hear what happened. "What did Dr. Roumalade say?" I ask when Aunt Hortense finally comes back to me.

"Not much," Aunt Hortense says.

I can't stand this. I head back to our kitchen. On the way, I see Jing come in. He didn't disappear the way the Sweeting servants did. Noah must still be here, too.

"Jing," I whisper, "I'll take care of Noah. I'll make sure he gets immunized. I promise."

Jing's face turns a baker's white. He wobbles as if I've kicked him in the shins.

"Dr. Roumalade has the antiserum. We have to get him to immunize everyone. Noah, too."

Jing's face sours. "The antiserum makes people sick."

"That's not true. I've had it, and I'm fine. So has Papa."

"No." The word comes out hard and angry.

"Papa wouldn't have immunized me if it weren't safe."

"People die from the immunization. I've seen it with my own eyes," Jing insists.

"I'm as fit as a fiddle, Jing. You have to put your faith in science. You know that," I say.

Jing scowls. What is the matter with him?

CHAPTER 32

Roumalade's Triage

Aunt Hortense and I look after Maggy. She sleeps fitfully, moaning in her sleep. She throws up, then curls up into a tight ball, kicking off her bedclothes. Dr. Roumalade and Uncle Karl are hunkered down in the Sweetings' kitchen.

"It's not the plague, Peanut. It's a stomach virus," Uncle Karl tells me. "Dr. Roumalade has done a thorough examination."

"She was touching the rats," I tell him.

"Doesn't mean she has the plague," Uncle Karl says.

Aunt Hortense looks at Roumalade. "Like I said, Doctor, let's err on the side of caution and make sure our Maggy is immunized. Jing, too."

"It's not necessary. But I will do as you wish, Mrs. Sweeting." He walks out of the house and across the cobblestone drive to the stepping-stones that lead to our back door.

In the big Sweeting kitchen, I help Aunt Hortense stoke the furnace and boil water for tea. I've seen Jing do this enough times to know how it's done.

"I feel terrible about the servants, Lizzie. How was I to know there were two kinds of serum? The other night, Roumalade was set to give something called Haffkine's antiserum to them. Apparently Haffkine's can kill you if you've already been exposed, and the side effects are terrible. Roumalade wasn't going to use his precious Yersin's on the help. And this from a man who swears there is no plague."

In a flash, it all makes sense. Why Mei jumped out the window. Why Jing wouldn't let Noah be immunized. It wasn't the same serum. It wasn't Yersin's. The servants were going to be given the risky immunization. And then I can barely breathe. "Maggy!"

I fly out the door and across the breezeway, up the stepping stones, and up two flights of stairs, three steps at a time, grateful for my long legs.

When I get to Maggy's door, I barge right in. "What are you doing?" I demand.

Roumalade's small eyes glare at me. "Taking care of your maid. Since you have single-handedly caused a frenzy of plague fear, your aunt has insisted that everyone be immunized. A little knowledge is a dangerous thing, Lizzie."

"Haffkine's or Yersin's?"

Roumalade's eyes register his surprise. "Who taught you to be so impudent?"

"What kind of immunization are you giving Maggy?" I demand.

"It's Yersin's. She's a maid. She shouldn't have it. But your aunt insisted—"

"Aunt Hortense paid for Yersin's," I say.

"I know that. Didn't you hear me? That's what I'm delivering." I see the bottle in his hand. He sticks the needle into the bottle, pulls the stopper back, and suctions the serum into the chamber.

When he pulls the needle out, I stare at the bottle. It's round, and the *IP* mark is missing. "You're not." My voice shakes.

"Of course I am."

I jump between him and Maggy. "Yersin's comes in a different bottle."

His nostrils expand. "You have no idea what you're talking about."

"I know exactly what I'm talking about. That's not Yersin's. Shall I get Aunt Hortense?"

He glares at me, the filled hypodermic needle in his hand.

"Get away from her!" I yell.

He takes a reluctant breath, then digs into his bag for the bottle with *IP* on the side and prepares another shot. I watch his every move.

He turns the label toward me. YERSIN'S.

"I'm only doing this out of professional courtesy," he says as he immunizes Maggy.

"You're only doing this because I'm forcing you and Aunt Hortense is paying." I stand at the door. "And now you need to immunize Jing and Noah. *With Yersin's.*" I knock on Jing's door. I know they're inside, but nobody answers.

"Jing," I call through the door. "You were right. The Haffkine immunization is a bad one. It can make you very sick, even kill you. Dr. Roumalade is here. He's going to immunize you and Noah with Yersin's. The immunization I had. The stuff that works. Aunt Hortense is paying for it. You have to believe me, Jing!"

I hold my breath. Jing doesn't respond. "There's not much time. Please, trust me."

Inside I hear muffled Chinese.

The door flies opens.

Jing's face is a mask. Noah's eyes ask me a hundred questions. I nod to him, trying to convey all I know without letting Roumalade see. Jing and Noah roll up their sleeves, and Roumalade fixes the immunizations, with me monitoring his every move. Yersin's for both. First he immunizes Jing.

"Wait a minute," Roumalade growls, holding Noah's arm. "Your aunt said *two* servants."

"No, she didn't," I lie with all my heart.

"I distinctly heard her. She said two. Maggy and one other."

Panic flickers across Jing's face.

"Shall we go ask her?" I stick my face in Roumalade's. "Then I can tell her how you were set to give Maggy Haffkine's even though she paid for Yersin's."

Roumalade glares at me, the Yersin's in the hypodermic needle. He gives the last immunization to Noah.

Billy's Secret

Roumalade has gone now. He left written instructions for how to take care of Maggy. Bed rest. Fluids. Cold sponge baths. Standard procedure for most diseases. He still won't admit Maggy has the plague. What is the matter with him?

Aunt Hortense and I do our best to care for Maggy as we wait and wait for Papa. When will he be back?

I've just run a cool cloth over Maggy's forehead when I hear John Henry's *clip-clop* on the cobblestones. I rush downstairs and practically jump onto Papa as he climbs down from the wagon. "Papa, am I glad—"

"Lizzie." His voice is strained. "Go to the Sweetings' house and stay there."

"What? Why?"

"Now." His voice is sharp.

"But I'm taking care of Maggy. I need to—"

"Lizzie!"

I run across the way and up the steps.

Papa calls out instructions to Jing. I don't hear what he says, but Aunt Hortense comes out and stands with me, her face white. Her shoulders shaking.

My father and Jing are unhooking the back of the wagon. Papa scrambles in and gently cradles a man in his arms.

Billy!

Jing is on one side, Papa on the other. Their arms are laced under Billy. He is half walking. Mostly they are carrying him.

"Was he in a fight?" I ask Aunt Hortense. Though I know Papa would not send me away if it were that.

"No," Aunt Hortense whispers.

I feel sick to my stomach. Maggy. Now Billy. Are we all going to die?

Billy is tough. He can fight anything. Papa is here. Nobody is going to die.

How did Billy get it? He had the Yersin's, didn't he?

Maybe it doesn't work.

Did he catch the plague in Chinatown?

I'm the one who made him go. Is it my fault?

But Maggy has it, too. She never leaves the house. The disease isn't just in Chinatown.

The rats gave it to Maggy, and Maggy gave it to Billy. Or Billy gave it to Maggy but it took longer to show in him. Or . . .

Papa says even when you know how a disease is passed from person to person, tracking the path of contagion is like chasing the wind.

But Papa is a wonderful doctor. He'll take care of Maggy and Billy. He'll make them well. I try to push out of my mind the memory of Papa caring for Mama.

Aunt Hortense takes my hand and holds it tight. We watch Billy, Papa, and Jing go inside.

Papa does not come out again. Jing hangs the yellow plague flag, then leaves a message in a basket at the Sweetings' that says we are to stay here.

"Wait, Jing!" I wave to him as he crosses back over the cobblestones. "Papa needs my help."

Jing shakes his head. "You stay where you are."

Aunt Hortense flies out of the house. "Elizabeth! Under no circumstances are you to enter a house with a plague flag."

"But I've already—"

"Do you hear me?" she roars.

"Yes, ma'am."

Noah. What about Noah? Thank goodness Jing and Noah had the Yersin's. And Billy? He had it in time, didn't he?

I get a chair and one of Aunt Hortense's sweaters and make myself comfortable on the balcony. I can't see Noah's window from here. But Jing is there. Jing will take care of Noah. Papa will care for Billy and Maggy. I write a note to Papa and leave it in the basket outside.

Dear Papa,

I've been taking care of Maggy already. Can't I come help?

Love,
Lizzie

P.S. Ask Billy if he took the Yersin's.

For dinner, Aunt Hortense warms up clam chowder for Uncle Karl and me. The bread is stale. We dip it into the soup to soften it.

"Any news?" Uncle Karl's eyes search our faces.

We shake our heads.

All night we worry. Nobody sleeps.

In the morning, Jing has left a note from Papa.

Dear Lizzie,

Billy is fighting. Maggy is doing better. You are to stay put.

Love,
Papa

"He's fighting. That's good, isn't it?" I ask Aunt Hortense.

Her hands tremble as she fits the tea cozy over the teapot.

I pace the balcony, my mind full of the magic tricks we did when we were little. Billy blindfolded catching the only red chicken in the coop. Billy tied up with a lead rope, untying himself with his teeth. Billy pulling bunny droppings out of a hat.

If the tricks didn't work, Billy would figure out how to make everyone laugh.

Even now with the fighting, he got a black eye and needed stitches. But he never got seriously hurt. And he won a lot of the fights, didn't he?

Nothing can happen to him. He's Billy.

I think about him at La Jeunesse dancing with the dark-haired girl in the crimson dress. All eyes were on her, but she only had eyes for Billy.

Does the plague flag hanging from our house mean our barn, too? I decide against asking and take the back way to our stable. I can't stand being cooped up at the Sweetings' any longer.

Up to the loft I climb, looking for Orange Tom. Maybe he came home with Noah. If Noah is still here, he will have written to me.

Sure enough, Orange Tom is prowling the loft. But when he sees me, he skitters down the ramp. I chase after him around the barn. He slips out the door and up to our house, where he sits taunting me.

I run all the way back to the Sweetings' kitchen, looking for food to bribe him. In the cold storage, I find anchovies. Outside with the stinky greasy fish in my hand, I look again for the cat.

Not on the porch. I go back to the barn. Not there. Around to the side yard. Behind the chicken coop. I finally find him under a garden chair.

I throw a piece of anchovy his way. His tail switches.

He walks lazily to it and picks it up in his teeth. I toss another. He watches it land, then strolls over and snatches that one.

One more anchovy and he's close enough for me to grab him by the neck.

But there is no thread on his collar. No message. Nothing.

When the brand-new motorcar gets delivered, I figure Uncle Karl bought it for Billy. He thought it might give him one more reason to fight this off.

Uncle Karl comes out onto the porch, his eyes on the shiny automachine. "That was nice of you," I say, and plant a kiss on his cheek.

He gives me a stony look.

"You got it for him, right?"

"No." His voice is gruff.

"But Billy didn't have the money yet," I say.

Uncle Karl's keen blue eyes lock on the motorcar.

"How'd he . . ."

"He sold it," Uncle Karl whispers.

"Sold what?"

Uncle Karl doesn't answer.

"What did he sell, Uncle Karl?"

Uncle Karl's face is crumbling. I've never seen him look this way.

"Not the Yersin's," I say. "He didn't sell the Yersin's."

Uncle Karl grinds his cigar into the ashtray so hard, the ends splay. "He did."

"No!" I shout.

I run down to the motorcar and kick the tires as hard as I can. I bang the brand-new doors with my fists until my hands hurt. That stupid, stupid thing. I keep bashing until I feel Aunt Hortense's arms around me. Her lavender smell.

"Lizzie," she whispers. "That's not going to help."

"How could he? He sold the Yersin's for this . . . this hunk of—"

"Lizzie . . ."

"Billy!" I holler as loudly as I can. "Why are you so stupid?" I'm sobbing now. I can't stop.

Uncle Karl turns his back. He walks inside.

CHAPTER 34

Polishing the Motorcar

The next day, I'm out there with a cloth, shining every last inch of that stupid contraption. Aunt Hortense comes out with me. "Tell him it's perfect, Aunt Hortense. I didn't scratch it. I hardly even put a dent in it," I whisper. "Tell him it's waiting for him. He has to drive it. We're all waiting for him to drive it. Tell him."

Tears flow down my cheeks. They drip down my chin.

"Tell him he's not stupid. Tell him he's the best grumpy brother in the whole world." I sob.

"I'll tell him, Lizzie." She dabs at her eyes with her handkerchief.

"Maybe if we get the girl in the crimson dress. The beautiful one he took to the cotillion. Maybe if he sees her out the window," I say. "She could be all dressed up, just like she was."

"Maybe." Aunt Hortense sniffs.

"She was beautiful, Aunt Hortense. You should have seen her. And the boys he wants to fight. Maybe we could set up a fight ring down on the driveway so he could see. And we can get him brand-new fighting clothes. And make a stage for him to do his magic tricks. And tools with lots of bicycles to fix and . . . and . . . Papa has to make sure Billy comes to the window. He has to see. Can we do that, Aunt Hortense? Can we?"

Uncle Karl is on the porch pacing. Aunt Hortense has moved her chair out here, too. We all want to be as close to Billy as possible.

This is where we are a few hours later when my father finally comes out of our house. He sinks down onto the kitchen steps; his head drops into his hands.

"No!" Aunt Hortense wails. She holds me close. "Not Billy. Not our beautiful boy. Please, please not him."

Uncle Karl goes back behind the stable to where the servants chop wood. We hear him with the ax chopping and chopping.

I watch our house as if I'm in the sky looking down. This can't be true. It isn't true. Billy will walk down the stairs as he always does, his pocket jingling from the nickels he earned fixing bicycles. He will grab a piece of Jing's pie, harness John Henry to the wagon, and off he'll go, calling me a pest and telling me no, I can't come along.

I hold my breath, waiting. Let it out and hold it again.

But Billy does not come down the stairs. Soon the black undertaker's wagon arrives.

CHAPTER 35

Sugar Water

Three days later, Aunt Hortense's new maids clean our house from top to bottom, Papa takes down the plague flag, and I move back. It feels good to be home—and awful, too.

Every time I walk by Billy's room, the emptiness haunts me. His room was full of him. It felt like him. It smelled like him. But now the room is quiet. The quilt, the fight posters, the boxing gloves unmoved from one day to the next.

I wonder how I'm going to get through this. When Mama died, it was Billy who kept me busy with the magic shows, the secret bareback rides, and the barn games. "Billy," I whisper. "Didn't you know how much I need you?"

Every day, I go to check on Maggy. Most of the time,

she's sitting up in bed, the parrot on her shoulder. Papa moved his cage upstairs. He said Maggy told him she wanted the parrot in her room. He was amazed. It's the first time Maggy has ever said she wanted anything.

Now when I walk into her room, Mr. P. chirps, "Maggy Doyle! Maggy Doyle!" like he's announcing her arrival at a cotillion.

I wish I knew why Maggy got better and Billy did not. Was it the timing of when she received the Yersin's? But Yersin's is supposed to be preventative. Does it lessen the effect of the disease once you get it? Did Papa give it to Billy once he got sick? The more I think about this, the more questions I have.

The day of Billy's service, I put on the black velvet dress Aunt Hortense bought for me.

Papa, Aunt Hortense, Uncle Karl, and I all drive in Billy's motorcar. Billy would have wanted this. We know that.

Jing is in the wagon with a few of the Sweeting servants who have returned. We are just about to go when Maggy Doyle appears wearing a dark dress no one knew she had. In the eight years she has worked for us, she hasn't ever worn anything but her uniform, and she has never left the property.

She climbs into the wagon with Jing.

At the church there are a few hundred people, most of whom I have never seen before. Everybody knows Uncle Karl's nephew died. Some people know it was the plague, and still they come. Everybody wants to pay respects. I sit next to Papa holding his hand. He has barely been able to speak since Billy died. His heart has been crushed. We listen to the minister say a bunch of things that don't feel like they fit Billy.

But only the people who love Billy are allowed to come to the cemetery after. As we climb the hill, Gemma runs to me and holds my hand. Gus stands by, looking tall and handsome in his black suit. Gus is smart and quiet and kind—so kind. My stomach flutters when I see him, but not as much as it does when I see Noah.

I stand by Mama's gravestone, and then we all take turns speaking about Billy. Uncle Karl talks about how clever he was. The beautiful black-haired girl from La Jeunesse says how gently he held her hand. Papa tells stories about when he was little and changed all the clocks in the house so he could have his birthday party all over again. Papa says he keeps waiting for Billy to do that now.

When it's my turn, I read my poem for him. It's the one time I don't cry.

Billy had big hands. He was wild and he was grand.
He taught me to land soft when I jumped from our loft.
He taught me the knack of riding bareback
And how to fight in the dead of night.
I couldn't learn Billy's charm or sew stitches in my arm.
But when he sawed himself in half, I was his staff.
And when I was blue, he always knew.
I can vouch he could also be a grouch.
But he had a way of showing up

Just when things were blowing up.
A million times he came to my defense with Uncle Karl
and Aunt Hortense.
Billy gave Papa a whole lot of woe,
And we will miss him so, so, so.

In the small cluster of Sweeting servants leaving the cemetery, suddenly I see a head I know well. Black straight hair and a white shirt. A square jaw and bright eyes. Noah! He brushes by me, pressing a note into my hand. We say nothing in the crowd of people. I feel the heat of his skin on my fingers long after he lets go.

Gemma's head whips around. "Lizzie, where are you?"

"Here." I wave one hand while slipping the note into my pocket with the other, and hurry back to the Trotters. I walk with them, Aunt Hortense, Uncle Karl, and Papa. Nobody has anything to say.

In the powder room at the Sweetings', I unfold Noah's note. *4 p.m. Sunday in the stable.* YES! This is the first time I've been able to smile since Billy died.

That night in our drawing room, Uncle Karl, Papa, Aunt Hortense, and I talk things out in a way we haven't before.

I pepper Papa with questions. Billy was younger and stronger. Shouldn't he have been able to fight the plague better than Maggy? And how did Maggy and Billy get it? Is Gus right, the rats spread the plague? If so, how, exactly?

Papa is in the big chair. He's leaned over, resting his

long arms on his knees. He shakes his head. "Those are my questions, too."

"We need to know these things," I tell him.

"She's right," Aunt Hortense whispers. Her voice is hoarse.

"I don't understand why Dr. Roumalade kept insisting Maggy didn't have the plague. Her symptoms were so clear," I say to Uncle Karl and Papa.

Aunt Hortense and Uncle Karl, sitting together on the sofa, exchange a look.

"His patients are railroad money, dear," Aunt Hortense says.

"So?"

"Word gets out we have the plague, people won't be taking the train to San Francisco."

"Nobody likes to lose money, Peanut," Uncle Karl says.

"But he's a doctor. He's supposed to take care of people, not worry about money." I jump up and start pacing. I'm too upset to sit still.

"No two ways about it, he behaved abominably," Papa says.

"Yes." Aunt Hortense's eyes are on Uncle Karl. "Dr. Roumalade used Yersin's to immunize himself and the patients who could pay."

"So he did believe the plague was here," I say.

"Who knows what he believes. But he certainly made a pretty penny on the Yersin's," Uncle Karl says.

"Oh no! That's not who Billy sold it to . . . is it?" I ask.

The room goes silent. Papa looks like he's going to be

ill, but it's he who answers me. "He sold it to one of his boxing buddies. A man who had been on the boat from Honolulu."

"Is that how the plague got here?"

"Apparently."

"Why did Roumalade say there was no plague?" I ask. "Wouldn't he have gotten more money for the Yersin's if he'd said the plague was here?"

"He was playing both sides. Keeping his wealthy railroad patients happy while making money on the side. Besides, he couldn't very well say the plague was here when the surgeon general of the United States said there was no plague," Uncle Karl says.

"Is that what they all believed?" I ask.

"Impossible to know," Aunt Hortense says.

"Why did you get upset about that monkey?" I ask Uncle Karl.

"Consensus was that the monkey, guinea pig, and rat business was a stunt. Dr. Kinyoun, the so-called wolf doctor, concocted the whole thing to save his hide. Nobody thought the quarantine was warranted. He wanted to prove it was. I didn't want to give credence to what everyone thought was pure nonsense."

"It wasn't much of a quarantine. There weren't any doctors or nurses," I say.

"Kinyoun had the power to call the quarantine, but he couldn't get the rest of the medical community on board with it," Uncle Karl explains.

"But he was right."

Uncle Karl sighs. "He *was* right. We know that now. But, Peanut, I'm in the news business, not the history business. I have to call events as they're unfolding. There wasn't a reputable doctor in the whole state who thought this was the plague."

"You know who else was right," Aunt Hortense whispers. "Hearst."

"Mary, mother of God, woman, do you have to bring that up?"

"Hearst printed plague stories to sell more newspapers. You did what you thought was right, Karl. You kept unfounded allegations out of the news." Papa's voice is quiet.

Uncle Karl stares at Papa. "I appreciate your saying that, Jules. Means a lot coming from you."

Papa nods. His movements are slow, as if everything he does is painful.

"Even with all that, why would Dr. Roumalade try to give Maggy the Haffkine's? He must have known she had the plague. Did he want to kill her?"

"Do you know for certain it was Haffkine's?" Papa asks.

"I know it wasn't Yersin's," I say.

"My bet is it was sugar water," Papa says.

Uncle Karl nods. "Even Haffkine's costs money. Roumalade must have figured a servant who has already contracted the plague is a lost cause. Better to give her the cheapest thing possible.

"Which reminds me, Mrs. Sweeting," Uncle Karl continues. "I got a bill from Roumalade. He charged me an arm and a leg for the Yersin's, which I was expecting. But his bill says he immunized three Kennedy servants. It was only Maggy and Jing."

Aunt Hortense's eyes flash to me. The look on her face is shocking. Does she know about Noah?

"That's right. Two servants," Aunt Hortense says. "But pay it anyway. I'm on that children's hospital charity committee with his wife. I'd just as soon not have trouble with Hillary Roumalade."

CHAPTER 36

Too Many Secrets

I'm helping Aunt Hortense write cards to all the people who sent flowers for Billy. We wear black and sit at a table in her sitting room with the big windows that open out to the balcony overlooking the garden. I watch her write. She has better handwriting than I do.

"Why do people keep secrets?" I ask her.

She looks up. "Because they don't trust each other, I suppose, although there are all kinds of secrets. Some are harmless. Some are not."

"It seems like there have been way too many secrets. I'm going to live the way Papa does. Straightforward and honest. No secrets."

"You are, are you?" She dips her pen into the ink.

"Yes."

She taps the excess ink from the nib. "In a perfect world, we wouldn't need secrets. But the world's a long way from perfect. Still, I try to be as straightforward as I can, which is a challenge, given who I'm married to."

"If Billy had told us what he was doing, if he hadn't kept it secret, we could have talked him out of it," I say.

She stops. "Billy was headstrong. He wasn't an easy one to sway."

"If only he were here, and I could convince him now. I know just what I'd say."

"Which is . . ."

"I'd tell him how important his life is to me and to Papa and to you and to Uncle Karl. I'd say he has to hold it gently in his hands as if it is the most precious thing in the world. And never ever trade it for money. I'd tell him money is only wrinkled old paper. It's nothing at all compared to him, compared to his life."

"I wish you could have told him that, too." Her eyes search mine. "Lizzie?"

"Yes, ma'am."

"When were you going to tell me that Jing has a son?"

I cough, almost choking.

"I saw him with Jing. They look so much alike, it wasn't hard to figure out." She runs her hand along the pen feather.

I remember how Billy said Aunt Hortense is more complicated than I give her credit for, but there are some things she'll never tolerate. Me dancing with Noah is one of them. I tread carefully.

"He's about your age, isn't he?" Aunt Hortense asks.

"Yes, ma'am," I say.

"But he's not working for anyone."

"No, ma'am."

She nods. "Why do you suppose that is?"

"He wants to go to college," I whisper. "Like me."

One carefully shaped eyebrow rises. I hold my breath.

She turns away. "Of course you'll need a proper education, Elizabeth, and then medical school . . . if you're going to be a doctor."

I gasp.

She looks back at me. "I wanted a different life for you. Your father wanted a different life for Billy. But that didn't work, did it? You'll have to"—she can hardly get the words out over the welling in her throat—"live your life your way."

"Aunt Hortense!" I jump up and throw my arms around her.

"My goodness, Lizzie." Her voice is husky. She takes out her handkerchief and tries to clean up her face. But as soon as she does, more tears come down.

At quarter to four, I check to see where everyone is in the house. Papa is in his room. He is still so sad about Billy that he can hardly eat. I know he will get through it, just as he did when Mama died, but right now it's hard. Maggy is on the porch knitting. She's almost all better. Aunt Hortense and Uncle Karl are at their house. Jing is in the kitchen adding sugar to a boiling pot of apples. The way he watches me, I know he knows that I'm meeting Noah.

"Lizzie," he says as I open the back door.

"Yes, sir." The word pops out of my mouth without me even thinking about it. Papa and Uncle Karl are always "sir," but never Jing.

Jing's shoulders pull back; his head rises. Our eyes meet. He doesn't try to make me laugh. He has no frog in his pocket, no quarter in his ear, no feather or stone up his sleeve.

He stirs the apples. "Your mama would have been proud of you," he says.

His words are warm inside me as I walk out to the barn. He has never said anything like this before.

Orange Tom lurks in the foggy darkening afternoon, his thick fur matted on one side, tail flecked with bits of leaves and straw.

I open the barn door. Noah stands petting Juliet's muzzle.

"Lizzie." He takes my hand. "I'm sorry about Billy."

The heat of his hand warms mine.

We start to dance. Our first steps are stiff; then slowly the rhythm builds. My hand feels solid on Noah's shirt as we circle the stable.

Noah steadies me. I don't care if I make a wrong step when I'm with him.

We float together, breathing in the sweet smell of alfalfa. Only Juliet watches, slurping her water. John Henry is asleep.

I don't want this to end. I hold on to every minute. The world is kinder with Noah holding my hand.

When he lets go, he crouches and pounces. He jumps back onto his springy legs and then up onto his hands.

One day, I'll see Noah perform his lion dance in his costume with all of his friends. For now, it's time to go. Aunt Hortense has come a long way, but I can't upset her. Not now. Not after all we've been through.

One day, things will be different.

One day, she'll understand that Noah is my friend.

"I'll be back soon," Noah says.

I nod.

By the chicken coop, I capture Orange Tom. He doesn't give me a chase this time. He simply allows me to scoop him up and carry him to my room. I write one last message. My hands shake as I wrap the red thread around the note.

University of California in 5 years

Noah,
Save me a chair.
I'll be there.
Lizzie

Glossary

	Transliteration	**Chinese Characters**
Friend	"pung yau"	朋 友
Hello	"nei ho"	你 好
Papa	"ba ba"	爸 爸
Thank you	"doh je"	謝 謝

Author's Note

Chasing Secrets is fiction. Lizzie and Noah's story is purely imagined. The account of the 1900 outbreak of bubonic plague in San Francisco was true. I tried to stick to the facts as much as possible, but I altered the timing of some events. I took creative license in extending the time between when the guinea pigs and the rat died and the monkey's demise. I moved up the forced immunization using Haffkine and only included one quarantine, when there were actually two. The chronology at the end of this section lays out the true dates of events.

THE CITY

"In 1900, white San Francisco was a sophisticated city of 350,000 people,"[1] many of whom were freewheeling, chock-full of optimism and bravado. Some had become millionaires nearly overnight, finding their fortunes in the Gold Rush, the railroads, the Comstock silver mines, or the sugar business. The city was suffering the growing pains of turning a Wild West mining boomtown into the Paris of the Pacific. And though it was the Victorian era, in San Francisco there were "fewer rules and regulations than in well-established cities back East."[2]

At the turn of the twentieth century, there were "only

about eight thousand cars in the country."[3] Many people did not welcome the new contraptions. One of the reasons people were seeking to develop this form of transportation was because of the pollution caused by horses. Manure, dust, and dead horses on the street were all big problems. But the first motorcars were quite primitive. In early auto races, a car was considered successful if it reached the finish line. The winner of the first American race clocked in at seven miles an hour.[4]

Street performers were also a big part of the vibrant city life. Though the Astral Dog scene was fiction, the idea came from a memoir by Malcolm Barker about late-nineteenth-century San Francisco that included this line: "A trick dog knows which girl is your soul mate."

CHINATOWN

Prejudice against the Chinese, who stood on the lowest rung of the immigrant ladder, was at its zenith at the turn of the twentieth century, and "Chinatown was the district San Francisco demonized."[5] Chinatown was its own city within San Francisco, an exotic ghetto crowded with twenty thousand Chinese Americans. Many white San Franciscans held the Chinese responsible for all manner of diseases and social ills.

"As long as times were good, the Chinese were accepted, but a late-nineteenth-century depression turned the tide. Formerly prized for their productivity, the Chinese now were cast as cunning and insidious job stealers."[6]

Chinese children were not welcome in public schools:

> The (Chinese) boys were sent to school; that is, to the Chinese school; they were not allowed to go to the European school. At that time, there was one public school of about four rooms, on Clay Street, between Stockton and Powell Streets, those in attendance being mostly Japanese and other races. . . . The Chinese boys went to their own school.[7]

This account makes it sound as though Chinese girls did not attend school at all. I did find other sources indicating that some Chinese girls attended school along with Chinese boys. Donaldina Cameron, who appears in this novel, was a real person known as the Angry Angel of Chinatown. She made it her mission to rescue Chinese girls who had been sold into slavery.

MEDICINE

Rudyard Kipling once said, "Wonderful little our fathers knew. Half of their remedies cured you dead." And that was certainly true of medicine in 1900, though it was a fascinating time, on the verge of epic change. Germ theory was in its infancy, yet many doctors did not understand—much less believe—the science behind it:

> To the San Francisco citizens of 1900—even to most practicing physicians—the new bacteriology was still a form of black magic: mysterious, dimly understood, untrustworthy and inferior

> to the laying on of hands and the observation of symptoms at the bedside.[8]

Hospitals were widely distrusted. Doctors routinely made house calls and performed operations on kitchen tables. Many barely made a living. Better to have your son be a blacksmith or a bricklayer than a physician.

Some daughters of doctors did accompany their fathers on house calls. One such girl wrote: "Whenever it was possible, he took me with him on his calls in the country. I was always eager to go: I loved just being with him."[9] And from the memoir of a country doctor: "When the roads were good and the trip not too long, I took my black-eyed little daughter with me."[10]

There were very few female doctors. And of course, women did not yet wear pants or have the right to vote, and they were often refused entry to bars, restaurants, and other businesses.

THE PLAGUE

Bubonic plague is one of the most feared diseases of all time, thought to be responsible for the death of one fourth to one third of the total population of Europe in the Middle Ages. It is generally* transferred from person to person via rat fleas. The fleas suck the blood of the infected rat. When the rat dies, the flea hops to a new host. The infected

* Pneumonic plague is a type of bubonic plague contracted by about 3 percent of cases. It is far more contagious than regular bubonic plague.

flea bites its new host and injects the plague directly into the bloodstream.

In 1897, Paul-Louis Simond discovered that rat fleas spread the disease. He published his findings, but his research had not yet been given the blessing of the scientific community. In 1900 the U.S. Surgeon General published a report stating that the plague was contracted by breathing contaminated air. Though incorrect, it was the prevailing opinion at the time.

Throughout history, there was anecdotal evidence that linked rat death to the plague. "An ancient Indian text the Bhagavat Puran, had, long before, warned people to leave their houses when a rat fell from the roof, tottered about the floor and died; for then be sure that plague is at hand."[11]

San Francisco rat fleas differ slightly from Asian rat fleas and are less successful at plague pathogen transfer. This may be one of the reasons the plague did not do as much damage in San Francisco as it did in other locations. Even so, the plague is mysterious. As author Edward Marriott stated, "If diseases have personalities, plague is an escape artist, a criminal Houdini."[12] How, for example, did the scourge of the Black Death finally end? Nobody really knows.

THE FIRST PLAGUE OUTBREAK IN SAN FRANCISCO

> On March 6, 1900, a Chinaman died of Plague in Chinatown and very soon thereafter others

> of his countrymen succumbed to the same dread disease. The local and federal health authorities were thoroughly alive to the situation from the start, but encountered innumerable obstacles in their efforts to control the disease. The story of how short-sighted commercialism connived with lying newspapers to deceive San Franciscans as to the actual presence and extent of the Plague is a black chapter in the history of this fair city which will never be given much space in a lay history.[13]

The wolf doctor, Dr. Joseph Kinyoun, was trained at the Pasteur Institute in the nascent science of bacteriology. He was able to extract the plague pathogen from the corpse of the first-known casualty and inject it into a rat, two guinea pigs, and a monkey. If the animals died, he believed it would confirm his plague diagnosis. But no one liked the arrogant, abrasive Dr. Kinyoun, and when first the rat and the guinea pigs and later the monkey died, it was easier to attribute the deaths to Kinyoun's intervention than to the plague virus.[14]

The partial newspaper account in the text on page 200 is almost verbatim from *Chung Sai Yat Po.* Below is an extract from the *Call.*

> After appearing in a continuous performance of three days, in a scientific farce, which proved to be a commercial tragedy to San Francisco, the

> Bubonic Board of Health, relying on the testimony of a rat, a monkey and a guinea pig, left the footlights, raised the quarantine of Chinatown and left the city to recover, as best it can, from the widespread damage inflicted upon its trade and every other material interest.
>
> What a spectacle the incident presents! The Chief of Police hurrying at midnight to rope in a quarter of the city; the Bubonic Board adopting the phraseology of grave emergency by bulletins that had "the situation well in hand" and in other terms promoting the belief that it had identified the plague and had given the pestilence a flying switch from the glands of a Chinese into those of a guinea-pig; the stolid indifference of the city; the inefficiency of the quarantine maintained by the Chief of Police, which it is said, Chinese boast of escaping by the payment of a dollar a head—all go to make a record of official imbecility, and worse that has not been equaled in the history of the city. It is enough to make the guinea pig grin.[15]

Still, clear evidence of the plague could be found. "In the Chinatown epidemic, eighty-seven dead rats, eleven dead of the plague, were found in the walls of a Chinese restaurant. Several cases of human plague had been traced to this place, but they immediately ceased when the rats were cleaned out."[16]

The Yersin versus Haffkine immunization question also closely hewed to actual events. The Yersin's did come from horses, and it was expensive. Medical personnel were given this immunization, which was thought to be more effective. The Haffkine immunization had significant side effects, and it was dangerous if injected into people who had already been exposed to the plague. There is now, however, some question about how effective the Yersin was—though that was not known at the time.

It is also true that the surgeon general "prescribed a mass vaccination of all the Chinese . . . [with Haffkine which] was violently unpopular in Chinatown."[17] And one girl did jump out the window rather than be immunized.[18]

CONFUSION AND DENIAL

Many people in both the Caucasian and Chinese communities had reason to deny the plague outbreak. San Franciscans were vested in the rise of their city. The railroads brought tourists to the jewel of the Pacific. Imports arrived and exports shipped from thriving ports. News of a plague outbreak would have brought the business of San Francisco to a grinding halt.

The Chinese feared scapegoating with good reason. The quarantine had been patently unfair. Any Caucasian person was allowed out of the quarantine area, whereas the Chinese were not. (Many San Franciscans believed only persons of Chinese descent could be infected by the plague, which was, of course, untrue.) Then, too, the Chinese feared that Chinatown would be torched, as had happened when the plague struck Honolulu.[19] "By Friday, it is hoped that we will know that this was not the plague. Otherwise what happened in Honolulu might happen to us."[20] Even before the plague crisis, there were people who actively campaigned to burn Chinatown.

Perhaps the only businesses to be glad for a plague crisis were the undertakers and the Hearst newspaper enterprise. Hearst realized a plague scare would be good for circulation, and he made the most of it. All of the other newspapers conspired to keep any real news of the plague out of their pages. "In a stunning admission on March 25, the *Call*'s editors admitted that they and the *Chronicle*'s editors had made a mutual pact of silence on the plague."[21]

It is impossible to know how many people died of the plague. Doctors routinely misdiagnosed it. "Most physicians' attempts to understand plague amounted to little more than wild fumbling, their theories born of prejudice."[22]

People hid their plague victims—either by shipping them out of the city hidden in barrels and boxes or via paperwork ruses whereby the cause of death was attributed to other diseases. Official plague death toll accounts vary from 250 to 280 people, but "to arrive at a better sense of the real numbers of deaths would require a careful biostatistical analysis of the unusual rise in deaths between 1900 and 1901 recorded as acute syphilis or pneumonia. . . ."[23]

"Chinese residents, concerned that their homes would be burned down, hid their sick relatives and then shuttled them out of the city in small boats at night. Sometimes when an inspector arrived before a body could be removed, a dead man would be propped up next to a table in an underground room, his hands arranged carefully over dominoes."[24]

ERADICATING THE PLAGUE

By 1905 the first plague crisis had subsided. Chinatown and surrounding areas had been scoured from top to bottom, which made them less attractive to the rat population. When the second San Francisco plague epidemic hit after the 1906 earthquake, there were few if any plague deaths in Chinatown. "Between the first [plague] epidemic in 1900 and the second in 1907, the role of the flea and the rat in transmitting plague to human populations was elucidated."[25] And the new surgeon general, Rupert Blue, was able to stop the plague through an extensive rattery operation, which aimed to trap and kill 1,200 rats per day.

Notes

1. Crichton, Judy, *America 1900* (New York: Henry Holt and Company, 1998) 28.
2. Barker, Malcolm E., *More San Francisco Memoirs, 1852–1899: The Ripening Years* (San Francisco: Londonborn Publications, 1996) 27.
3. Crichton, *America 1900,* 15.
4. *Library of Congress* http://www.americaslibrary.gov/jb/progress/jb_progress_autorace_1.html (accessed November 26, 2014).
5. Craddock, Susan, *City of Plagues: Disease, Poverty, and Deviance in San Francisco* (Minneapolis: University of Minnesota Press, 2000) 55.
6. Chase, Marilyn, *The Barbary Plague: The Black Death in Victorian San Francisco* (New York: Random House, 2003) 9.
7. "The Virtual Museum of the City of San Francisco," sfmuseum.net/hist9/cook.html.
8. Chase, *The Barbary Plague,* 46.
9. Hawkins, Cora Frear, *Buggies, Blizzards and Babies* (Ames: Iowa State University Press, 1971) 72.
10. Hertzler, Arthur E., M.D., *The Horse and Buggy Doctor* (Lincoln: University of Nebraska Press, 1938) 126.
11. Barnett, S. Anthony, *The Story of Rats: Their Impact on Us, and Our Impact on Them* (Australia: Allen & Unwin, 2001) 32.
12. Marriott, Edward, *Plague: A Story of Science, Rivalry and the Scourge That Won't Go Away* (New York: Henry Holt, 2004) 230.
13. Marion, Jay, *A History of the California Academy of Medicine, 1870–1930* (San Francisco: Grabhorn Press for the California Academy of Medicine 1930) 85.

14. Chase, *The Barbary Plague,* 47.
15. *San Francisco Call,* 3.11.1900, http://cdnc.ucr.edu/cgi-bin/cdnc?a=d&d=SFC19000311.2.80
16. Todd, Frank Morton, *Eradicating Plague from San Francisco: Report of the Citizens' Health Committee* (San Francisco: Press of C. A. Murdock, 1909) 21.
17. Chase, *The Barbary Plague,* 48–49.
18. Chase, *The Barbary Plague,* 50.
19. Chase, *The Barbary Plague,* 19.
20. *Chung Sai Yat Po*, March 7, 1900 p. 1. (in Chase, *The Barbary Plague,* 19.)
21. Chase, *The Barbary Plague,* 54.
22. Marriott, *Plague: A Story of Science, Rivalry and the Scourge That Won't Go Away* 13.
23. Echenberg, Myron, *Plague Ports: The Global Urban Impact of Bubonic Plague Between 1894 and 1901* (New York: New York University Press, 2007) 231.
24. Sullivan, Robert, *Rats: Observations on the History and Habitat of the City's Most Unwanted Inhabitants* (New York: Bloomsbury, 2004) 157.
25. Craddock, *City of Plagues,* 18.

Chronology

1900

January 2. San Francisco dock. The steamer *Australia* arrives from Honolulu, where the plague has struck. Rats from the ship are believed to run up the sewers to Chinatown.

January–February. Chinatown. Chinese observe an inordinate number of rats dying.

March 6. Chinatown. A man dies from the plague in San Francisco. First known case here.

March 7. Angel Island. Dr. Kinyoun, the wolf doctor, injects plague from the dead man into a rat, two guinea pigs, and a monkey.

March 7–10. First Chinatown quarantine.

March 12. Angel Island. The rat and the guinea pigs die.

March 13. Angel Island. The monkey dies.

March–May. More deaths from the plague.

May 29–June 15. Second Chinatown quarantine.

June 14. The governor of California (Governor Gage) and the deans of three medical schools sign a manifesto that states there is no plague in San Francisco.

1902–1908

November 1902. The city begins to try to get its rat population under control.

February 1905. San Francisco's first plague outbreak is declared over.

April 18, 1906. The San Francisco Earthquake and fire rip the city apart. In the ensuing days, rats gain a foothold again and the plague returns with a vengeance.

November 1908. The plague is finally vanquished in San Francisco.

About the Author

Gennifer Choldenko is the *New York Times* bestselling and Newbery Honor–winning author of many popular children's books, including *Notes from a Liar and Her Dog, If a Tree Falls at Lunch Period, Al Capone Does My Shirts, Al Capone Shines My Shoes, Al Capone Does My Homework,* and *No Passengers Beyond This Point.* She lives in the San Francisco Bay Area, where she hopes never to see a rat. Dead or otherwise. Visit her online at choldenko.com.